# DEMON IN MY VIEW

# Demon in My View

# Tom Henighan

A BOARDWALK BOOK
A MEMBER OF THE DUNDURN GROUP
TORONTO

Editor: Barry Jowett
Design: Alison Carr
Printer: Webcom

**Library and Archives Canada Cataloguing in Publication**

Henighan, Tom
Demon in my view / Tom Henighan.

ISBN-13: 978-1-55002-656-6
ISBN-10: 1-55002-656-9

I. Title.
PS8565.E582D44 2007 jC813'.54 C2006-904613-1

1    2    3    4    5        11    10    09    08    07

Conseil des Arts du Canada    Canada Council for the Arts    Canadä    ONTARIO ARTS COUNCIL CONSEIL DES ARTS DE L'ONTARIO

We acknowledge the support of the **Canada Council for the Arts** and the **Ontario Arts Council** for our publishing program. We also acknowledge the financial support of the **Government of Canada** through the **Book Publishing Industry Development Program** and **The Association for the Export of Canadian Books**, and the **Government of Ontario** through the **Ontario Book Publishers Tax Credit program** and the **Ontario Media Development Corporation**.

Printed and bound in Canada
Printed on recycled paper

www.dundurn.com

| Dundurn Press | Gazelle Book Services Limited | Dundurn Press |
|---|---|---|
| 3 Church Street, Suite 500 | White Cross Mills | 2250 Military Road |
| Toronto, Ontario, Canada | High Town, Lancaster, England | Tonawanda, NY |
| M5E 1M2 | LA1 4XS | U.S.A. 14150 |

*To Michael Carroll and Robert Powell, two superb students who have become my teachers and friends.*

From childhood's hour I have not been
As others were; I have not seen
As others saw; I could not bring
My passions from a common spring.
From the same source I have not taken
My sorrow; I could not awaken
My heart to joy at the same tone;
And all I loved, *I* loved alone.
*Then* — in my childhood, in the dawn
Of a most stormy life — was drawn
From every depth of good and ill
The mystery which binds me still:
From the torrent, or the fountain,
From the red cliff of the mountain,
From the sun that round me rolled
In its autumn tint of gold,
From the lightning in the sky
As it passed me flying by,
From the thunder and the storm,
And the cloud that took the form
(When the rest of Heaven was blue)
Of a demon in my view.

Edgar Allan Poe, "Alone"

# CHAPTER ONE

It was not a village, hardly even a hamlet; merely a cluster of shacks and shabby outbuildings that skirted a deeply rutted road beside a stretch of bare, open field.

A cold day in spring, for the afternoon sun had vanished behind a barrier of thick, grey clouds. An old woman, sweeping the steps of the largest building, stopped to rub her skinny hands together and blow on them.

Very slowly, she tilted her head sideways, as if she had heard something in the distance. She stood listening, staring off in the direction of the gently sloping, wooded hillside. Suddenly, she ran from the large building — a rickety old schoolhouse surrounded by a few benches and crude play-structures. She scampered across the road and disappeared inside a tarpaper shack no bigger than an outhouse.

Inside the school's single large classroom, a crowd of boys and girls of various ages, from about ten to eighteen, were singing verses they knew by heart: an old hymn, although delivered in the style of a rap song. Mr. Koenich, the teacher, a grizzled, desperate-eyed, worn-out looking man dressed in a brown, shabby garment like a monk's, insisted they finish each school day in this manner. He explained that the terrifying visions and beseeching words of this song had been handed down from the days of the great terror, and that it was necessary to remember them, and to pray every day, if they were to prevent evil forces from destroying everything they valued.

*God's wrath has thundered down*
*On every village and town.*
*The fields dry up and burn*
*The demons take their turn.*
*The bikers ride from hell*
*The priest will toll a bell.*
*The mountains run with blood.*
*In our old neighbourhood*
*There's nothing left to steal*
*There's nothing worse to feel.*
*Save us from the fire*
*And terror in the night*
*Save us from the plague*

*Help us fight the fight.*
*Yeah, Lord! Yeah!*
*Show us the righteous way*
*Help us in our pain.*
*Bring the good times back again!*

The students had sung — rapped out — these words often, and even though they enjoyed the pulsing rhythm of their own delivery, they knew the words were powerless to change anything. And because they were eager to be released from school, they always chanted them very fast, and with a certain careless ease.

Young Toby Johnson, at the back of the classroom, who had the best voice and the keenest ears of them all, was not speaking, but listening. He shifted uneasily in his place, fists clenched against his well-worn overalls, eyes pressed tightly shut. He was trying hard to identify a distant sound, the same sound that had caused the old woman to throw down her broom and flee to shelter.

Toby didn't move, although he wanted badly to run to the window and look out. The distant sound, much closer now, and clearly audible, was a roaring of powerful engines. Within seconds it became bursts of thunder that shook the walls of the schoolhouse and reverberated among the buildings outside. The students' singing faltered a little, and the room seethed with excitement.

Mr. Koenich raised his hickory stick and nodded to his burly teaching assistant. The class stopped singing, and the students whispered and nudged each other, stirring uneasily in the places. The assistant rubbed one thick hand against his black leather jacket, pushed himself off the high stool where he sat dozing, and quickly fetched his shotgun from the corner of the room.

"Only fire at them if they attack the school," Mr. Koenich ordered. "Students! Lie flat on the floor. Keep still, and stop your fussing about. Toby! Get away from that window!"

"But, sir, my dog's out there. I've got to fetch him inside."

"You'll do no such thing. Lie down with the rest of the students and keep your mouth shut. Your dog can take care of himself."

Toby stretched his body on the floor, closing and unclosing his fists in sheer frustration. A pretty girl lay down next to him and began to stroke his left arm and shoulder.

"Don't take no mind, Toby. Ranger will hide out from them all right."

"They'll kill him if they see him, that's the problem."

"Two motorcycles!" the teaching assistant reported from the window. "It's a couple of the Reardon boys. They're buzzin' in and out the schoolyard. Just having some fun, I guess. Just passing through."

The younger children, laughing and calling out to each other, were wriggling and writhing on the floor, imitating the roar of the engines and making jokes about the Reardons. Only a few of the older ones, who knew something about the biker family, seemed frightened. Toby wanted desperately to look out the window. The walls of the room shook and vibrated. Suddenly, the roaring subsided, and in the silence, in quick succession, they heard two gunshots.

"Now, now," Mr. Koenich mumbled. "We don't want any of that. Just ride your damned Harleys out of town, boys. Go off somewhere else for your target practice."

"That dog's out there. That's what they're shooting at!" reported the assistant.

Toby jumped to his feet and sprinted across to the window.

"Get away from there!" Mr. Koenich sprang across the room and made to grab him, but Toby eluded him, and pressed his face against the window pane.

"They're leaving!" the assistant told Toby. "Look, they're heading straight out of town."

"They'd better!" Toby said grimly. "If they hurt Ranger, I'll kill them. I'll kill them both!"

There was a murmuring behind him; the students were getting up. The crisis was over, but one of the class jokers shouted from the far corner.

"Why you gonna kill them, Toby? Gonna give your daddy a little more burying business?"

"Never mind that stuff," Mr. Koenich warned the boy, but the class was already breaking up in laughter.

"There goes Toby, back to the homestead," a wiry, scruffy ten-year-old shouted. "How's your old man? Still burying all those corpses in the woods?"

Toby turned angrily on his skinny, sneering antagonist, then seemed to think better of it. He shrugged his shoulders, fumbled with the door latch, and at last shoved it open. Cold air struck his face. He shivered, and walked across the porch to the rickety steps.

He cupped his hands around his mouth. "Ranger!" he shouted. When nothing happened, he put his fingers to his lips and whistled loudly. A sharp, clear, and penetrating sound that all his classmates always envied.

He waited, but the dog didn't come.

"Go see your crazy father! Go see Old Shovelbeard!" a girl called out.

"Old Talby's got a bone shop!" jeered another.

But Toby was hardly listening. He whistled again, and then stood waiting, gazing up and down the deserted road. Fear possessed him, the sinking, sickening feeling that permeates your mind and soul when you begin to assume the worst.

Mr. Koenich had come out on the steps. He put an arm around the boy's shoulder and told him, "Don't pay them any mind, Toby. Look, he's coming after all! The Reardons didn't do him any harm."

A great black Labrador had sprung out from behind a nearby building and was racing straight for the school steps.

Toby ran forward, grabbed the dog, and hugged it. He bent down, stroking Ranger's smooth brow and back.

"It's gettin' real late, boy," Toby whispered. "We've gotta get back to old Talby."

Toby heard voices and shuffling steps, and felt the presence of his teacher and many of the students behind him milling around on the porch and watching him. But he didn't turn around. He moved off quickly, while Ranger sprinted back and forth, running circles around him. They hurried down the rutted road, followed it past the shabby fields, then slowly climbed the hill and entered the deep woods.

# CHAPTER TWO

That was not the last time, at the end of the school day, that the taunts of his classmates would scald him. To escape them, the boy would cut away from the road at the old quarry, cross the fields through Froats's barren apple orchard, and enter the forest that grew thick at the boundary of his father's almost impenetrable acres.

There he would come to the pool that lay between the giant boulders, stopping to look at his own image in the voiceless water.

If he had looked clearly, from a greater height or a different time, he might have discovered himself: a boy of about seventeen, tall and thin, with golden wavy hair and blue eyes of a deep sad intensity. But from where he gazed down he could see only the masks: the face of a pilot, an athlete, a daredevil rider or soldier, each of which floated there for an instant, then dissolved in a blur of pure light and shadow.

Slowly he would go on, up the narrow trail between the pines, toward the "homestead," as everybody called it, toward the small cabin in the clearing at the top, the cabin with a sagging roof and rotting foundations, the clearing strewn with wood his father had pillaged from the ruin of the sugaring shack. He would stop a minute and watch a black squirrel scurry out of the open trunk of the Chevrolet, its tail brushed red with rust from the rotten guts of the machine. Then he would listen for sounds coming out of the deep woods that spread away on all sides of the homestead, half-afraid he would hear the roar of the Reardon gang's motorcycles, the guns of the hunters, or his father's shovel at work somewhere near — burying a dead animal, or perhaps a human corpse left over from one of the skirmishes in the maple grove.

Mostly, if it were summer, the cabin would be empty, the door standing half-open, and, as the boy came near, Ranger would bound out to greet him, a few burrs stuck in his short coat, and would paw and scratch at the old canvas bag in which the boy carried his schoolbooks and pencils.

Inside, it was dark, and the red eye of the fire, in all seasons, would gleam on the oilcloth, and light up the faded photographs hung in old frames on the rough walls, or glitter across the rows of beer bottles his father had found in the woods and stacked everywhere in pyramids around the cabin. Then the boy would listen until he heard the nuzzling and bleating of the goats through the window. He would fetch himself a mug of milk and dip into it a crust of stale bread, and sit reading the pamphlets that had been left in the cabin long ago, when people still believed that things could be made better. They were little folders of cheap yellowing paper telling about the end of the world, how Jesus Christ would save every believer, and how the earth would be a paradise at last, when all the wicked had been exterminated by the power of a wrathful God.

And then he would feel upon him the eyes of the dead in the photographs, his mother's most intensely of all. Those blue eyes he had never forgotten — though the old snapshots had curled and faded. And the gazes of vanished relatives haunted him too. People he could hardly remember, or knew only by hearsay: Uncle Isaac and Aunt Martha, Cousin David and the Harrison girl from the Grantley concession, and the twins, Ruth and Sam, who had disappeared after some recent violence.

Then Ranger would press in and lick the boy's hand for a crust, and Toby would toss away the soggy bread and watch the dog scramble after it, sometimes knocking down his father's carefully propped-up row of shovels, picks, and spades, shaking the bottles and making a terrible clatter in the small cabin room.

Among the seasons, to which he was very close, Toby liked autumn the best, even though it meant he had to go back to school. He didn't mind sitting all day in the big schoolroom at Carson's Corners, though he shrank from the whispering and pointing. He hated how his classmates seemed to notice every frayed edge and patch on his clothes (although his father took them for repair from time to time to the widow Marston). Above all, he hated the way they made fun of his father, how they imitated his shuffling, bent walk, or screamed with sharp laughter when they mimicked the old man's way with a shovel or a pick.

Why did his father have to be so old, with a long, ragged beard that trailed down almost to his belt buckle? Why did he have to wear the same faded grey work clothes, the same shabby coats, and a cap that was worse than the battered headgear of old Top Hat, the crazy black man who lived in the hills?

Worst of all, why was he the one who had to bury the dead? Why couldn't he plant corn or potatoes like the rest of the farmers, instead of digging in hidden places and laying to rest the poor creatures of God's earth: the killed, spoiled deer, the slaughtered hawks and wild geese, even the groundhogs, not to mention the travellers or passers-by — mutants mostly — who had the misfortune to starve in the woods, or who had been shot by the hunters or run down by the Reardon gang because they got in the way during one of the motorcycle races?

"Crazy Talby," the children and young folk whispered, and sometimes shouted, and Toby would think of the name when he watched his father some mornings, bent over the stove, where he always made the same hard, flat pancakes for breakfast, scraping them carefully from the skillet, and spooning out three, always three, for Toby, while the coffee settled down and the milk boiled up right beside it.

Father and son would sit opposite each other at the small table and Toby would stare down at the worn, shiny oilcloth while Talby said grace with elaborate and resonant piety. And Toby would sometimes look up, fascinated by his father's hoarse voice, by the way his beard flowed down in the honey bowl, by the stray tufts of hair at the old man's wrists and nostrils.

Only rarely would the boy take courage to look straight into his father's deep-sunken watery grey eyes, yet when he did, those eyes would hold him for long seconds with a mildness and innocence he could hardly name but felt steadily, like a pleasing gentle pressure, in his chest and stomach.

And on those autumn mornings when the leaves were just turning gold or russet, Toby would be awakened by the sound of the hunters' guns, the clear, faintly echoing *crack crack crack* tossing him round on his bunk. He would start up, cloaked in shadows, and see that his father had already gone. And once or twice the boy crept out, before his father returned to make breakfast, and watched in the woods, and saw the hunters. His father had told him the story of Nimrod from the Bible, but these were only men from a nearby village: storekeepers and handy-men who walked stiffly, warily, despite their neon orange hats and store-bought guns. With faces frozen and eyes glazed, they stopped now and then to pass a small flask from hand to hand, peering anxiously around them, and holding hard to their weapons, as if their bodies had gone rigid in a state between fear and desire.

The bikers were different. They would come roar-ing up the trails, hacking at the trees with hatchets and long knives, firing their shotguns at random, four or five at once rolling a captured girl underneath the maples, sometimes dumping a victim in the under-brush, a mutant whose face had been blasted away, a farmer who had taken pity on one of the fugitives.

This had gone on for as long as Toby could remember, although his father once told him it had started after the war (the war against terror, the eter-nal war), and now continued uncontrolled, at least in the country. And the boy knew that the bikers both hated and respected his father — hating him, as the hunters did, because he cared for what they tried to destroy, and respecting him, despite themselves, because he was not afraid.

But sometimes the boy was afraid, because he knew in his heart that things could not go on in the same way forever. Once or twice the bikers had come to the shack and smashed all the windows and thrown a corpse into the well, and the hunters had tried to shoot Ranger. There were swastikas painted on the last of the sheds, and once a goat with its throat slit was nailed up to the cabin door. So when the attack finally came, it was something expected, like a storm seen unfolding across a broad placid valley.

# Chapter Three

On a clear day late in spring, during one of the last six weeks of school, while Toby was sitting dreaming in one of Froats's apple trees, chopping at a grey, brittle branch with his jackknife, he heard the roar of the motorcycles.

Within minutes two riders appeared, cutting deep tracks in the soft road. Toby shrank back.

It was Mal and Whit Reardon, the oldest of the brothers, burly riders in black leather and jackboots — Mal with a shining bald head and a shotgun strapped to his back, Whit in a fur vest-coat, and wearing the green-tinted goggles that, even at some distance, gave his eyes a cold, snaky cast.

While Toby held his breath, the two riders stopped in the road just opposite the orchard. They rocked to and fro on their Harleys, gunning their engines, the sharp rasping sounds like snarls of anxious irritation.

Leaning their heads close, they exchanged a few words, then glanced once or twice in his direction. Toby thought he saw them smiling, and half-expected them to come roaring across the field after him. Suddenly, they did move, but wheeled away down the road and soon disappeared behind a line of trees.

The boy slid slowly down the grey, twisted trunk. Had he mistaken their look? Had the riders come there to find him, to make sure of where he was? But to what purpose?

In a sudden panic, Toby looked around. The main path to the homestead lay behind him, twisting up through the new sprouting brush, through the maples and birch, to the clearing. But there were other paths, and beside one of them his father was surely at work. He and Toby had heard the bikers riding all night, and there had been gunfire and shouting and low moaning cries until dawn.

Toby started to run. He dodged through the trees, leapt a ditch, crossed a small scrubby field, and bounded away up the narrow track, breathing hard as he jumped over loose stones and small trenches gouged out by the spring rain.

The familiar woods and its features flowed past his eyes like pictures on a moving screen: there was the pool, spilling water; the ancient split rock; the ash tree, still thin-leafed and bare; the lone tamarack.

Out of breath, he burst into the clearing and stopped short. The cabin lay peaceful, untouched. A thin thread of smoke rose from the chimney; swallows wheeled out of the shed. The woods were almost silent, except for a thin, distant buzzing of bikes muffled down to a faint, bee-like hum.

"Ranger?" the boy called in a tentative voice

He walked slowly up to the cabin and entered. He felt, as always, the sense of a quiet sanctuary within, everything in its place, and the fire lit. The dog, though, was nowhere in sight.

Outside, the boy raised his voice in a series of calls; then he listened, half-expecting to hear the patient, steady thrust of his father's shovel at work in the near-by woods, afraid that the silence might explode with the roar of machinery.

He called at the top of his voice, and at last heard a faint bark. Within minutes he was tracking the sound, beating down through the stiff underbrush that lay to the north of the homestead. There were a few trails there where the bikers, on certain nights, ran their quarry. Mal and Whit Reardon, he knew, could have circled and entered the woods from the road on the other side.

Toby pushed on, his glazed eyes steady. Nonetheless, he felt fear at the bone. Then the dog barked, not far off.

Toby crashed through a small stand of pines and saw the first body: a thin old man in the overalls of a farmer, sprawled under a branch. Part of his head had been shot away and one hand, twisted and crushed, reached across the dark needles, the fingers poking down at the earth.

Toby bent over, retching. He clawed violently at the branches, slowly circling the place, trying not to look at the shattered head. He knew it was Jacob Brent, the grandfather of his friend David. They had killed him, but surely he had never harmed anyone, never threatened the bikers.

It was horrible. Toby struggled forward, beating back the branches, trying to reach a clear space. Then, as he turned to run away, he tripped over the second body: a woman, shot through the chest, bound roughly with half-rotten rope to the stump of an old pine. Her face was white, waxen, grotesque. She was clearly dead. Toby did not know who she was.

For a few moments the boy stood there, overcome by the terrifying stillness that surrounded the place. Then, with a start, he realized that the dog was barking furiously close by, that a fresh breeze had stirred up the branches, that his own heart was beating wildly, though the bodies lay in a silence nothing human could break.

It was what his father had wished to spare him: this vision of the unburied dead; this violation of the flesh. The boy, overcome by deep sadness, went mechanically forward.

He wandered dazedly out on the path. With its deep-scored ruts, it ran like a raw strip up into the trees. The earth seemed to crumble beneath him; here, tires had flung stray pebbles and sheered off thick clods of caked earth. Plunged deep in the soft green bank was his father's best shovel.

From behind, all at once, something leapt. Startled, Toby grabbed and held Ranger, and the dog rubbed its nose on his cheek. He kept jumping against Toby and barking.

Talby's voice called out his son's name.

Fifty feet up the trail, Toby saw the old man, crouched down among a small stand of birch trees. Some of the branches had been hacked at and snapped off; they tapered down around Talby like the bars of a cage. He bent over, pressing his eyes with his hands, moaning softly.

Toby ran forward. His father stretched out awkwardly to embrace him. His eyes, slits of pain, oozed flecks of white foam. Toby kicked away a prisoning branch and clung hard to his father, who straightened up, revealing his torn clothes and bruised cheeks and forehead. The boy hugged him close.

"I'm blind," said the old man. "They've blinded me."

He wrenched himself away, brushing at his eyelids with his stubby gnarled fingers. A grey-white foam ran in the hollows underneath his eyes; he blinked helplessly.

"Quick, Father!" Toby felt the tears scald his own eyes as he pulled the old man along the path. The dog criss-crossed wildly ahead of them. Toby half-dragged, half-coaxed his father up the sharp slope to where a clear stream bubbled out from the rocks.

"Bend over!" the boy commanded, pressing his father down close to the stream. Cupping the water in his hands, he splashed a rough handful in the old man's squinting eyes. Talby cried out in protest, sputtering and wheezing, and rubbing his eyes all the harder.

"Don't do that!" the boy cried, and scooped up the water all the faster. Ranger jumped up and down beside them, barking loudly and catching the splashed water with his tongue. The old man sat blinking, drenched, his hands moving restlessly at his side. The boy hurled more and more water in the old man's face.

"Enough!" cried the old man at last. He sat there, his torn grey worksuit soaked through, his eyes blinking, clear of the foam, flashing grey.

Toby reached out and gently touched his father's eyes, as if trying to make them focus on him, but they looked somewhere beyond, their clear, grey intensity blurred.

"They've blinded me. Shot some foul stuff in my eyes," the old man said, in a harsh, trembling voice. "Now who will bury the dead?" He bowed his head, seeming to retreat into his own misery.

Toby would not believe it. He jumped up, crying, "No! No!" and began hurling stones at the trees. "You've got to see, Father. You've got to!" His sobs broke the clear air; the dog whined at his heels.

But after a few minutes the boy felt the anger go out of him. He looked down at his father, whose glance failed to meet his. Then Toby felt a great weight on his shoulders, something pressing the breath and the life from his body. Slowly, he sank down on the turf where his father sat mumbling, still wrapped in his own thoughts.

"It was the Reardons that did it," his father said. "They care nothing for the old laws."

"I'll kill them. I'll kill them if it's the last thing I do," the boy said, and his voice cracked with passion, his hands making impotent fists at his side.

Talby took hold of his son's arm. "Come," he said softly. "You must help me get home."

# Chapter Four

They walked up through the woods, the boy leading the way, holding tight to his father's wet sleeve. Toby balanced the old man's shovel on one shoulder. There was no sound of intruders, no machines, though the birds started up in quick bursts as the two of them trudged by. Easing the old man through the pines, around damp rotted stumps, past glazed, mossy boulders that lay across the path, Toby led the way back. He said nothing about the two corpses he had stumbled on just before finding his father, but when they drew near the place of the murder, he saw how old Talby paused for a moment, turning his sightless eyes on the bodies, as if some deep instinct in his soul had made him aware of them.

The home clearing was quiet; smoke rising from the cabin. While Toby groped at the door, his father stood by helplessly.

"Am I never to see my house again?" he asked in a trembling voice.

The boy helped his father into the low bunk bed near the fireplace. Quickly, he boiled water, threw in some tea, let it cool. Then, taking great care, he used clean cloths to bathe the old man's eyes.

"It's no good," Talby said, "I can't see." And he lay back groaning on the bunk.

Mechanically, Toby went about making supper for them both. After a while Talby ceased to complain and lay quietly staring up at the roof. Toby did not know what to say to him. There was a terrible anger in his heart; he wanted revenge, to strike out at those who had done this to his father. Every time the boy slipped out of the cabin — to fetch wood, or to look around the clearing with an anxious, nervous glance — his father's voice pursued him. "Don't leave me alone, Toby. Don't leave me alone now."

Toby sat beside his father, took hold of one of the old man's gnarled hands, and attempted to distract him. "I don't know what to do, Father. Tell me what to do. I don't understand anything. You told me once you would explain everything. You would tell me about how this awful world happened."

Talby groaned, and for long minutes he was silent. "I can't face it, Son." He said at last. "What's the use of talking about those evil days?"

"You said you'd tell me when I was of age," Toby cried. "'All the Old Believers pass on the word,' you said. Remember that? Now I have to try to be of age whether I am or not. You've got to help me understand."

His father groaned again; he started to sit up, then collapsed back on his bunk. After a few minutes, however, he began to speak.

"There's a trunk by the bed here. It contains some of your mother's special clothes and things, you know that. But there's a smaller box inside it. The key for that's hung up there behind the clock. Fetch me the key now, Son. You're right — it's time to pass on the scripture copy, the commission, to you, to set you on the path. It wasn't supposed to be until you were twenty-one, but that's all changed now."

Toby opened the large chest — which wasn't locked — rummaged through the piles of clothes, old slippers, sweaters, and gloves, and at the bottom found a wooden box, about the size of a briefcase. He handed the box to his father and fetched him the key. Talby fumbled, opened the lock, and handed the box back to him.

"You'll find what you need to know in there," his father sighed. "I pray it helps you, because I have an idea that you'll soon have to go away from here."

"I'd never leave you, Father. I'll take care of you. I'm strong and I can do chores — anything. And I'll get the Reardons, too, for what they've done to you."

"*Vengeance is mine, saith the Lord,*" warned old Talby, quoting the ancient scripture. "Now open the box and read the papers."

Toby laid the box on the table and carefully lifted the lid. Inside was a bundle of papers, tied with a frayed red ribbon. There might have been a hundred sheets altogether. Some few, he noticed, had been written by hand in a fine old cursive; others were covered with elaborate drawings. The rest of the sheets were pasted over with clippings from newspapers and magazines.

Toby turned to the handwritten pages first. He laid the document flat on the table and began reading.

## THE PACT OF THE TRUE BELIEVERS

*These are the writings of the true believers, set down in the year of our Lord 2050, when the great troubles caused by evil men finally set the world in flames.*

*We are gathered together today to make this pact among ourselves, and between our people and the Lord, so as to preserve the teachings of God into the future, and to protect the world from the lawless, the unholy, and the demons that walk the earth in many disguises. In order to do these things, to keep our ancient commission, we agree to act as follows:*

*First, to obey the old commandments, not to kill or steal, or to practice abominations.*

*Second, to preserve the teachings of the Book and to pass them on to our children, especially our first-born sons, whom we shall cherish and instruct in the ways of God.*

*Third, to pray and conduct services, so as to beg the mercy of the Lord on humankind, and to further the day when all shall return to the path of righteousness.*

*Fourth, to avoid violence and machinery, to cultivate the land, and to bury the dead.*

*Fifth, to keep counsel together toward that day when we can re-inhabit the promised land given to our fathers, and make it bloom and flourish.*

*Sixth, never to lose hope.*

*Seventh, never to give up the faith.*

*Eighth, never to compromise with evil.*

*Ninth, never to consort with the demonic ones, the witches, the wizards, the magicians, the mutant souls, and the murderers who use hell's machinery against God's people.*

*Tenth, never to be corrupted by the foreign strangers, the Old Europeans, or the new men from the East. To rest solely in the hope of a new America.*

*God Save Our Promised Land of the North!*

Toby read these words a few times over. Some of the statements he understood, but other things remained obscure. He turned to the other pages, which were scrawled over with minute instructions for services and ceremonies, for rituals and prayers. The drawings and diagrams seemed to relate to these. The actual printed pages, however, were quite different. These were in fact a collection of newspaper and magazine clippings, carefully pasted on the blank sheets, and they offered a much more vivid, though still very fragmentary, picture of past events. Most of the dates were missing, as if whoever had compiled the file had stopped thinking of events taking place in time, and the latest date — 2073 C.E. — indicated that most newspapers had ceased publication after that. The striking headlines, however, compelled the boy to read what remained of the stories at once.

**RADIOACTIVE NIGHTMARE. NUCLEAR REACTORS GO OFF. THOUSANDS FLEE NORTHWARD. TERRORIST SABOTAGE SUSPECTED. ARRESTS WIDESPREAD.**

**PRESIDENT JONES ASSASSINATED IN MILITARY COUP. VICE PRESIDENT FLEES TO EUROPE. CANADA REFUSES TO RECOGNIZE NEW U.S. GOVERNMENT. CHINESE MOVE INTO HAWAII.**

**STARVING MOBS STORM CALIFORNIA MANSIONS. LOOTING IS WIDESPREAD. GOVERNOR FLEES TO MEXICO WITH STATE FUNDS.**

INFLUENZA STRIKES AGAIN. PANDEMIC LEVELS IN CALGARY AND VANCOUVER. THOUSANDS DEAD. SARS NIGHTMARE CONTINUES IN ONTARIO.

RELIGIOUS PACIFISTS CHOOSE THE NORTH. OLD BELIEVERS ASK FOR ASYLUM IN CANADA, POINT TO VIOLENCE AND CORRUPTION IN U.S.A. GANGS THREATEN TO WAYLAY THEM AT THE BORDER.

CANADA CLOSES BORDER WITH U.S. SHUTS DOWN ALL IMMIGRATION FROM SOUTH. POINTS TO LAWLESSNESS, CRIMES OF FUGITIVES.

CANADIAN GOVERNMENT SEEKS NEW ALLIANCES WITH EUROPE AND CHINA. CHINESE DEMAND "TRADING ENCLAVES" ON CANADIAN WEST COAST.

PM KILLED IN "SUSPICIOUS" CRASH. GOVERNMENT CRISIS DEEPENS. BIKER GANGS CLOSE IN ON CAPITAL. RESIDENTS FLEE TO QUEBEC WILDERNESS. PROVINCIAL GOVERNMENTS UNDER NEW STRESS TO "GO IT ALONE."

Page after page Toby read, overcome by a frenzy of curiosity. "How are you doing?" Talby asked from time to time. "Tell me what you're reading." But the boy asked his father for patience, desperately trying to piece together the chaotic and violent past.

Some of what he read he understood. There had been much talk about such catastrophic events among his older schoolmates, and many references to the dire events of those days by his teacher. But Mr. Koenich had obviously left out much. Either he didn't know the whole story, or he was withholding it from the students, perhaps fearful that a true and complete knowledge of the violent past would depress or corrupt them.

After reading the newspaper accounts, it was clear to Toby that this country he lived in, once called Canada, had long ago collapsed under the pressure of violence, terror, plague, and unwanted immigration from a ruined and decimated United States. He knew that there was a great union of nations far away in Europe, and that China ruled all the East and part of the west coast of America. Even though — as rumour had it — Old Europe and China themselves had suffered revolutions, plagues, and pandemics, they scorned this land, which was known to those civilized places as the "lost world" — a region of violence and anarchy that few outsiders wished to penetrate. The two great world states, east and west, were busy trading with one another, attempting to deal with their food and health crises, trying to gain economic advantages. They had chosen to ignore — at least for the time being — the "lost world."

It was rumoured, however, that some companies from overseas were prospecting in certain areas, that secret mines had been opened in the east and north, and that deals involving guards and "protection" were being made with some of the biker gangs. Yet neither Toby nor a single one of his friends had ever seen anyone from "the outside world."

Now, as he put together what he had garnered from the fragmentary narratives with the information he had picked up in Mr. Koenich's classroom, Toby began to understand what had happened decades before, in the middle of the 21$^{st}$ century. In those days, it was clear, the greed of the rich had triumphed and the poor had been cast aside. Governments had become short-sighted and cruel, religions preached violence, and terror seemed the only answer to the hopelessness that lay heavy on large portions of mankind. North America had become the enemy, the chief target of the impoverished and exploited, and soon, out of fear, treasured freedoms eroded on the home front, and the whole continent turned into a place of secrecy and weapons. The population, intimidated by their own suspicions, and worn out by many false alarms and rumours of war, no longer saw the enemy as alien, but denounced their own countrymen, their neighbours, and their friends. No one was to be trusted; everyone spied on everyone else. But despite the government's ruthlessness, some great national shrines were desecrated, famous buildings were destroyed, and people feared more and more for their lives. And so, at last, the army took possession of the state.

The stories told how guerrilla bands had formed a resistance, how unthinkable weapons were unleashed, and how the environment was poisoned. Communications broke down; the government ceased to have power. The Four Horsemen — war, conquest, pestilence, and famine — seemed to ride across the land. There was no law but the law of violence and reprisal. Thousands died, and thousands more fled to the north, to old Canada. But the newcomers engulfed that country with their own miseries, until it, too, collapsed under the pressure of violence, plague, refugees, and subversion.

Soon after that the mutations began. No one was sure how they started. Perhaps the massive pollution had caused them, or dangerous chemicals that had been foisted upon the public, or stolen and misused by the desperate. Whatever the cause, children were born, seemingly human but very different in body shape and in mental processes from ordinary folk, and after many of them had been murdered, the mutants banded together. They hid themselves from the majority and began to plot against the others, for they began to think of themselves as superior. They called themselves the special ones, the Elect — and indeed, they had rare gifts. They formed a secret commonwealth within the crumbling state. They practised their own form of worship, but outsiders charged them with evil practices and told tales of black magic, of human sacrifice and satanic rites.

Toby's eyes widened as he read this, for he had heard many rumours about the mutants, of whom he had seen but a few, and those harmless. Now he learned, too, about the origin of the bikers. They had started as mere outlaws in the long-ago world, but after the troubles, they were supplemented by ex-soldiers and by many from the disbanded militias, and so the gangs became very powerful, and broke free from all restraints. Theirs was the law of the strong, and sometimes they hunted down the mutants, and sometimes they made alliance with them against the righteous, the Old Believers.

On and on Toby read, but his mind swelled with images of horror, he felt sickened at the failures of the past, and at last he threw the papers aside in sheer despair.

"What is it, Son?" his father asked. "The truth is very bitter, I know, but you must preserve it for those to come — for your own children."

"Yes, Father."

Toby sat silent at the table, his head bowed and cradled in his hands. A terrible weight had descended on him. He knew what kind of land he inhabited, what kind of people he might expect to find in the world beyond his father's homestead.

"What's the use, Father?" he spoke out at last. "What's the good of resisting? You and I, the Old Believers, we're just powerless. The bikers and the mutants have the weapons. We're finished before we even start, and that's the truth of it."

His father groaned in seeming despair, then, with an effort pushed himself upright on his bunk and cried out.

"No! No! There's always hope. We have to trust in God's providence. Too many of the others did not believe. They fell away; they lapsed into shamefulness. But we returned to the old laws, we embraced the Book. We swore the oath of Christian brotherhood; we refused all violence. We buried the dead and prayed for the guidance of the Lord. We waited, we prayed for deliverance, we kept our commission."

"But, Father —"

"I know, I know. It all seems hopeless." The old man fell back on the bunk, his words became reflective.

"Now I can't see, I can't do my duty to the dead. I have to lie here, crippled by my affliction, and wait until the bikers come and kill me. Like Job, I'm cast down. I cry out to the Lord, but despair has a grip on my heart."

Toby listened helpless, close to tears. He knew that the Old Believers were fast disappearing from the land. Who would fulfil the law and bury the bodies of their kinfolk? Who would solace the poor and the abandoned? Who would condemn the rituals of the mutants, the violence of the bikers? It was neither in his heart nor in his power to take on such tasks. He could care for his father, but he could not embrace the Book in the same way, with the same conviction. He knew this, but said nothing, and after a while, when the fire had died down to embers, he bade good night to old Talby, carefully put away the all the sad papers from the past, crawled into his own bunk, and went to sleep.

# CHAPTER FIVE

He awoke to the smell of fresh pancakes; sunlight flooded the room. Toby rolled over, yawned, stretched his arms. Then suddenly, darkly, he remembered and threw back the covers.

"Father!" he cried out. His hopes leapt, then died as he saw the old man grope and fumble, prying up the pancakes from the overheated skillet.

"Here, let me help you."

The boy sprang from the bed. Within minutes they were sitting down to breakfast together. But his first impression had not been entirely wrong, Toby decided, for his father seemed lively and happy, not at all sunk in the gloom of the previous night.

"I've had a good dream," the old man explained as they sipped tea and dipped the last of the pancakes in honey. "I have to tell you about it, because it concerns you."

Puzzled, the boy leaned across the rough table.

"In my dream an angel came to me," Talby explained quietly, a kind of glow in his voice, as he carefully sipped his tea. "He took me by the hand and showed me my cousin, John Wilson, another Old Believer, who lives some ways east and south of Apple Valley. As soon as I saw John's face I remembered the five hundred dollars in gold coins I lent him some years back — money that will come due this spring. Your mother made me save that money and bury it, but when Cousin John needed it for his daughter's dowry, I sent it to him. The angel told me I might get a treasure still. With that money, maybe I can get a cure for my eyes. There must be —," and here the old man swallowed hard, "there must be a good surgeon left somewhere. There's just got to be! And if that fails, maybe I can hire someone to help us in our work."

Talby was silent for a moment. In the face of his father's new hope, Toby could not understand why he himself felt so sad.

"What did the angel look like?" was all he could think to ask.

Talby pressed his hands to his eyes, then said, almost as if he was ignoring the boy's question. "I'd forgotten that nothing, except death itself, can take away the sights of my dreams. It was wonderful there, all the things I saw!"

"But you can't remember what the angel looked like?"

"Of course I remember what the angel looked like, boy. He was dressed all in white, with a great sword bound round his waist. He had shining blue eyes and blond hair. He was a beautiful creature, that angel. And he mentioned your name, Toby, that he did! He said you were to go over to the country beyond Apple Valley to fetch the money from John Wilson and bring it back here, safe and sound!"

The boy felt a kind of excitement tingle his scalp and his fingertips.

"Me?"

His father groped, shook his head in frustration, and finally took hold of the boy's shoulders.

"You must go right away, Son. There's not a moment to lose. I know you won't fail me." He paused, hearing Ranger barking at something outside. "Why is that dog making all that noise?"

"But how can I go off and leave you, Dad?" asked Toby, ignoring Ranger's calls. "The Reardons might come back. And how will you feed yourself? Anything could happen. I just can't pick up and leave you."

In his heart, Toby knew that the journey frightened him. In all his years he had never been far from the homestead. To go out into the world — to leave his father all alone and blind — was more than he had courage for. He wanted to run and hide in the back of the shed, in the darkness, where he had sometimes concealed himself when the sounds from the woods grew too painful.

Toby felt his father's fingers tighten on his shoulders. Twisting away, he turned, knocking over a stacked pyramid of bottles. A wild clatter followed. He burst through the door and stopped short.

"Toby!" his father's voice followed.

A man stood a few feet away, a great hulking figure who seemed to take up all the space in the clearing and to absorb the dazzling sunlight with the sheer bulk of his presence.

Toby gazed on the stranger, hearing his father's voice as from a distance, or as from a deep well. The boy did not turn but kept his eyes on the newcomer.

He was very tall, but also bulky and powerful, and he exuded the calm grace of a great, powerful cat. He was dressed in black leather trousers and jacket, the latter buttoned up to the neck and secured by a small bright red scarf. His heavy black leather boots seemed planted in the earth; he kept clasping and unclasping his gloved hands, touching the criss-crossing belts and deep pouches at his chest. Above the man's shoulders, just visible, was one wing of a crossbow, a quiver of bolts, and a backpack. On his head, set back at an angle, he wore an old battered top hat. His face was clean-shaven, with high cheekbones and fine sculpted lines, wrinkled and friendly, though his eyes glittered coldly. His skin was as black as mulberry bark washed by rain.

Toby started to cry out, but the man put a gloved finger to his lips and stepped forward. The boy shrank away, and heard his father struggling at the doorway behind him.

"Toby! Toby!" the old man called nervously. "Where have you got to?"

"It's all right, Talbot Johnson, there's a visitor here," said the stranger in a deep, steady voice. Ranger came bounding across the clearing, circled once round the newcomer, and settled down quietly. Toby looked from his father to the man. The stranger's voice, though it had a musical quality in it, was not really like the voices of the black men he knew. The boy wondered, could this be Top Hat, the hobo, the outcast of the woods, this man who looked more like a biker or outlaw?

"I've travelled a long way, but I believe that we're kinfolk, old man," the stranger said. "My name is James White. In the old days I was a postman; now I live by guiding and hunting. I had a dream the other night, when I was on my way across Apple Valley — I come from the country beyond there. In my dream I was told that if I came here I would find a distant cousin — Talbot Johnson by name — who might have some use for my services. Did the voice speak the truth, or have I wasted this part of my journey?"

The old man came forward, groped, and found his son's arm.

"Would you be related to the Whites over at Twin Forks?" Talby asked in a slow and hesitating voice.

"The same," the man replied. *How could he speak such a lie?* Toby wondered. But the man did not appear to be lying. He looked benignly from the boy to the old man and calmly brushed the dust from his jacket and trousers.

The old man thought for a minute, twisting his head as if he were trying to force his useless eyes to see, then he said quietly: "Come in, friend, I want to hear more about the dream that brought you here."

The next few hours were an agony for Toby. They sat at the oil-clothed table, among the photographs and the piled-up bottles, his father's sightless grey eyes seeking out the stranger. The big man was hunched over, his grizzled short hair shining like black lambswool, his sensitive hands reaching out for the bread and the cheese, as Toby's father heard out his dream and then recounted his own. And at intervals, Talby would turn to where his son sat, his stubby hands touching his rough beard, and murmur some phrase such as "Isn't that right, Son? Isn't this just an act of providence that our kinsman should come now?" And Toby, hypnotized by the sight of the visitor's crossbow and backpack, carefully set down by the door and, crowned with the battered old top hat, would in turn murmur some weak assent. But a vagabond from the woods, a stranger!

Toby was silent. He simply could not interrupt the flow of his father's excitement, nor could he account for his own confusion, caused by the way the visitor, for all his strangeness, put him at ease. He would turn his head with a wink, drawing a cautioning finger up to his lips, all the while nodding sincerely at Talby's animated presence across the table, so that the boy began to feel there was no menace toward the old man in the stranger's masquerade.

At last, the bargain was made; it was decided that the visitor would accompany Toby to the country out beyond Apple Valley, to John Wilson's homestead, to fetch the payment in gold that was owed. And by this time Toby was glad he did not have to go all the way through the deep woods alone, though he was far from fully trusting the stranger, and still wondered whether this was a trick to get Talby's money.

"But Father, how will you take care of yourself?" the boy burst out, nearly in tears, as they were almost ready to depart. "And who'll see to burying the dead and keeping the old laws while we're gone?" He thought of the Reardons and his anger swelled up. Then Jim White's calm voice spoke reassuringly from the doorway.

"Last night, on my way here, I came on two bodies in the woods. I gave them a decent burial, though I had only the small shovel I carry in my pack. As for your food, Talby Johnson, I've got a stock of unleavened bread in my satchel. I'll leave you seven loaves of it, all ready to be heated up. Sprinkle one loaf every day with a little water, and heat it gently in the fireplace. By the time you've eaten the seven loaves, you should have been repaid what's owed you."

Talby fumbled across the room and took his visitor by the hand. "I feel my son is safe with you, Jim White," the old man said. Then he stood back, his head bent at the rustling of the newspaper, as the black man set the wrapped parcel of loaves on the table.

At parting, the boy clung a long time to his father. The old man's beard touched his cheeks, and Toby, very gently, reached out to caress Talby's sightless eyes. The boy then spoke very quietly to Ranger, and proceeded to tie him up so as to prevent him from coming after them.

Jim White stood with the woods stretching away behind him. "Look for your son in seven days," he said, and whirled away, just as Talby shouted back at him:

"What's the good of telling a blind man to look? Take care of my boy, that's all I ask."

He ran his hands through Toby's hair, as the boy turned and saw, through his tears, Jim already striding away.

# CHAPTER SIX

Their path led south, down from the homestead, traversing the old concession road and then cutting across country. It ran through the endless overgrown tangle of what had long ago been the cleared fields of farms, across Indian River, still sluggish with decades of pollution, and then over the remains of the superhighway, which had once linked the various parts of the region. They might meet wild animals, hunters, or one of the roving motorcycle gangs, Jim White explained. "Even mutants," he added with a sharp look. They must keep under cover whenever possible, and move with all speed in order to be back as quickly as he had promised.

They had not been travelling more than an hour, and were pushing through a tangle of scrub cedars, past the burned-out ruins of an old stone farmhouse, when the dog caught up to them, trailing the long length of rope, which was half coiled around his neck and frayed at the end where he had chewed it through to get free.

"Well, I guess we're stuck with him," Jim White told the boy, who sliced off the rope with a single stroke of his jackknife. Ranger rolled once on his back and then plunged on ahead through the bush.

The first night they camped by an ancient railroad embankment, a dark mound that curved out of the woods and was studded with fragments of broken bottles, twisted fragments of discoloured metal, and turfed over with thick couch grass.

Jim White made a small fire and toasted slabs of bacon on a stick. He fried some bread in the grease and they ate sandwiches and drank hot tea. After making two beds from cut boughs and laying out for the boy the single ground sheet he carried in his pack, Jim White sat for a while, his back against a tree, smoking a cigarette and reciting, or half-singing, a long poem about a journey to the stars. The boy did not understand some parts of the poem, but hesitated to interrupt, and after several long, soothing minutes of the recital, his eyes made tired by the low, flickering flames of the campfire, he fell asleep.

He was awakened by rain falling very gently, almost a faint mist, on his cheeks. The boy rubbed his eyes and watched the dog, who sat comfortably by the smouldering fire, chewing a bit of bread.

A sudden whine and a thud brought Toby from his lethargy. He sat up, tossing his blanket among the shining leaves. A small feathered bolt like a spike quivered in the base of a nearby cut elm. Jim White strolled across the clearing to fetch the arrow.

"Want some breakfast?" he asked quietly, nodding at a pot that sat on the low fire. Toby helped himself to porridge, burning his mouth with the hot gruel. Once up and on the trail, however, he felt better, tossing a stick for the dog and swinging from bent birch trees until Jim White had to caution him about the noise.

They trudged along faintly rutted tracks that had been traced long ago by the ploughs of vanished farmers. They crossed tangled fields, and made their way past ruined farmhouses, broken silos, and half-gutted outbuildings. On the morning of the third day, just when the boy thought they would go on forever, they came out of the scrub woods and saw the Indian River, a broad sluggish stream, curving away into the featureless distance.

For some time, at Jim's insistence, they hid and watched from the sheltering trees. Toby held the dog while Jim White explained that they must now follow the river west to the place of crossing. Toby stared across the stream, noticing how the water's oily green surface created a rainbow of sad iridescence. In the distance he heard the faint purr of engines and the whine of a siren, a sound that his father had sometimes imitated and explained when he was recounting some of the terrors of the old days.

Despite the sunlight, Toby shivered, for he detected a strong odour of gasoline mingled with that of rotting fish — a smell rising from the river and from the dark oozing banks that enclosed it. Jim White, his face grim, pointed their way to the west and they began a march along the desolate banks where a few gulls scavenged, rising lazily, as the dog charged upon them.

Some hours later, toward noon, they slipped around a bend in the stream and Toby stood wide-eyed, staring across at field after field of tangled metal, a labyrinth of battered car roofs, jutting frameworks, red rusted chassis, crushed cabs, and tires stacked down to the water. These acres of junked vehicles spoke of ruin and collapse, of the death of the old ways, the old transportation, and they caused Toby to shake his head in wonder.

"The Dump of Despond," Jim White informed him. Then, with a wave of his hand, he added, "But also our bridge."

And Toby saw how the hulks of the wrecked cars had at one point been dragged, God knows how or by whom, down into the river, so that it was possible to walk over the sluggish current without immersing one's boots in the filthy water.

"We'll eat lunch on this side and then go on," Jim told him, leading the way along the bank to where a grim, half-circular cairn stood some distance from the car-bridge. Toby followed, relieved and at the same time a little disturbed by the absence of any other travellers, though from behind them, just faintly, the dim sirens still sounded.

In the sheltering cairn, Jim White slipped off the improvised strap that had held his top hat on the march, and put down hat, pack, and weapons while he set about building the lunch fire.

Distracted by the sight of the dump, Toby wandered aimlessly down to the river. The cracked windows of the half-submerged vehicles, leaking effluent from the scum-stirred river, shone darkly, like the tiny sluice gates of some hidden cloaca. There was no wind; the sunlight seemed to lie heavily on the stagnant water.

Toby sprawled out on a rough, stony outcropping, and picking up a few loose pebbles launched them one by one at the nearest car. Suddenly, the dog barked furiously, right at the boy's ear.

Toby turned slowly and saw the snake — a thick-bodied sidewinder, faintly slicked with oil along its blotched length. It slithered up out of the water, its slit eyes unblinking. Smoothly it coiled on the flat lower rock; the dog barked incessantly, but Toby was still able to hear the snake's sharp breathless hiss. He saw the banded tail vibrate, the broad head draw back as if to strike, while the dog pranced foolishly close to the snake, snarling and bounding in maniacal energy, as if it had already been bitten and was yelping in pain at its tormentor.

"Ranger!" Toby feared for the dog. He scrambled back, clutching at the loose stones, then hurling them toward the reptile. It coiled away. From behind him, Toby heard the voice of Jim White, faintly calling. He stretched his arms out for the dog and lost his balance. With a cry he went down, sliding helplessly forward, banging his knees on the rock. The river came up at him, like a black mouth suddenly opened; one hand struck warm flesh; he clung to the dog's flanks. His left boot dipped down in the water.

He froze, eye to eye with the snake, which had coiled round to face him. The rattle's buzz dinned in his ear. Fixed by the serpent's cold stare, he could scarcely breathe or even swallow. The tail moved like a vibrating arrowhead, the dog's hot breath was on his cheek. At the same time he felt the fingers of his right hand close round a smooth, heavy stone.

The dog leapt away, springing up higher and increasing its wild din of barking. The boy was aware of a figure standing on the rock above the dog. The stone in his hand seemed to put strength in his arm, in his body. Very slowly, he slid his legs in, pulling back from the snake, which coiled there, its full three-foot length held in perfect poised menace.

Then, swaying ever so slightly, the boy stood up. His knees buckled. He raised the stone high up over his head, holding fast with two hands. The snake whiplashed toward the dog. The boy brought the stone crashing down.

The snake writhed and twisted. The boy sprang away, clawing at the rock in vain for another suitable weapon. On the mud-smeared bank he saw a short length of rusted pipe and took hold of it, whirling round. He was aware of Jim White above him, poised with his crossbow. The snake fluttered crazily; suddenly, the boy saw its beauty, rainbows of light on its smooth skin, but at the same time knew he must strike to complete the act he had begun. He smashed at the creature repeatedly with his improvised weapon. The blows stung his hands; rust showered down on the stony earth. Seconds later, the snake lay battered and still.

The dog went on barking and prancing, nuzzling close to the dead reptile, turning it once with its paws. Jim White, crossbow in hand, stepped carefully across the rock. He stood gazing down, turned to the boy with a serious look, but said nothing. He stooped and picked up the snake; the dog whined a little, then drifted away along the embankment.

The boy stood waiting, half expecting that Jim White would throw the snake in the river, but the black man instead held it out to him and said quietly: "It's yours to keep, boy. You killed it."

Toby tossed away his bent piece of pipe, brushed his hands on his jacket, and took the snake, wincing, feeling the oily slick of the scales at his fingers. Inert in his hand, the thing was heavy; sunlight flashed on its crushed head.

"Bring it up to the fire," Jim White said quietly.

They sat together within the small circle of stones. The flames of the lunch fire seemed to melt away in the noon brightness. Jim White took the snake from the boy, smoothing its gashed skin, then with his knife and his fingers he pried open the tightly shut jaws. The white fangs shone menacingly.

Jim took a wide-mouthed flask from his pack and hooked each fang in turn on the lip, his fingers squeezing tightly on the head as he did so. A pale yellow liquor dribbled out of the snake's jaws. Then Jim set aside the flask, and as the boy looked on with wide, staring eyes, he slipped the jackknife from his belt and began to cut the snake, first scraping and tearing away the skin and then cutting off long strips of the grey-white flesh and setting them carefully aside. At last, he drew out of the snake's body some of the internal organs, grey revolting handfuls, and dropped them into a pot beside the fire.

"Waste not, want not," Jim White said, flashing a white-toothed smile at the boy's solemnity.

He threaded the snake meat on a thin stick he had cut for the purpose and began to cook it over the fire, at the same time hanging the pot from another stick jammed between two stones, so that, in a few minutes, the flames beneath set the contents sizzling.

After a while Jim took the pot from the fire and handed a skewer to the boy. "Taste it," he said, and when the boy hesitated he added, "It won't kill you, though you killed it. A hunter should taste his game."

Toby chewed gingerly on the hot, sweet flesh of the snake. He did not want to finish his morsel, and looked uncertainly at Jim White. Jim was pouring the boiled entrails into a second flask, which he carefully capped and then set beside the first. With a gulp, the boy swallowed the snake flesh.

Jim looked up at him. "That's good," he said gently, "but it's not necessary to eat any more. Have some bread and soup instead while I tell you a secret about this snake."

Obediently, the boy helped himself to a large slice of bread and a bowl of hot onion soup. While he ate, Jim White spoke to him in a soothing voice. His eyes were turned toward the glittering junk fields beyond the river.

"I know what you want, boy: the thing that's been in your heart since your father's blindness," he said.

"You want revenge. To get the Reardons, to hurt them because they hurt your father. You think that's your heart's duty, that somehow it will give you satisfaction — make you a man."

Jim paused, and without looking at the boy, tossed a stick on the fire.

"Well, maybe that's so, boy," he went on, seeing Toby's self-conscious look. "Some people think that way. But now that you've killed one of the snake spirits you might want to ask yourself: does it make you feel like a man?"

Again he paused, and the boy, too, looked away to the river. The sunlight gleamed coldly on the tops of the half-sunken cars. For a moment he wanted to cry out, to protest that the snake had gone after the dog, that he had struck out only in defence, but he caught himself up, hanging silent because he knew that, after all, Jim was not accusing him. And also he knew then that the man was right: the anger about his father had been smouldering in his heart ever since they had left Talby back at the homestead, blind and nearly helpless,

"Things have a purpose," Jim White said, picking up one of the flasks. "The serpent is dead, but with its venom we can maybe find a way to the treasure."

Toby looked at him, wondering. Did he mean the money John Wilson owed his father? The boy did not understand, but Jim, without further explanation, continued.

"You're right to worry about your father. He's been sore stricken. Yet I have a hunch this will help him."

With a gentle motion he shook up the contents of the second flask as if he were mixing some precious brew.

They finished lunch together in silence. Then Jim White scattered the embers of the fire and they packed up everything and walked on down to the river.

# CHAPTER SEVEN

Leaping from car top to car top, the dog several times nearly slipped into the black stream. Finally, Toby grabbed Ranger by the collar, and, when they reached a place where the thick scum had washed over the metal and made for a treacherous smoothness, he waited for Jim White. Jim came along behind, took hold of the boy's hand, and steered boy and dog to safety.

On the far side of the river, the dump stretched away for some miles. There was a path winding through it: a thin, muddy track fringed by rough grass, bramble, and stinging nettle. The swelling thickets looked strange, shooting up among the shining acres of twisted metal, old tires, and half-rotten mouldy upholstery. Occasionally, a steering wheel rose above a wall of smashed fenders. There were rusted-out licence plates nailed up to stumps, and bleached white bones — the bones of dogs or squirrels — here and there among the broken glass. Yet much of the litter of metal was concealed by spring's first wild outburst of greenery.

After a while, they emerged from the dumping ground and entered a monotonous flatland, an area of broad, scrubby fields and stunted trees. That afternoon's march seemed endless. They stepped across clogged ditches and ragged, overgrown furrows then circled old stumps and a few dilapidated shacks surrounded by broken and rusted bits of farm equipment that lay like steel traps in the rough soil. They paused to rest in places where the grass seemed fresh and free of nettles.

As the hours passed, Toby seemed to grow detached from his body. He moved like a sleepwalker, his legs heavy, his senses dulled by the repetitive scenery. His fight with the snake drifted through his mind like a dream. Yet his reverie was broken at last as Jim White paused, pointed ahead, and indicated with a gesture that the boy should stop and listen.

Toby stood still and heard the low sound of engines, a whirring and droning that slowly sharpened and grew louder. With a meaningful nod, Jim led him cautiously forward.

After a while they left the field path altogether, moving off into a small wood, sliding between tree trunks, or hurrying across broad open clearings. All the time the racket grew louder; once or twice they heard gunshots.

Toward sunset they found shelter in a ruined silo, sharing a frugal meal and keeping watch on the path, which lay a bare twenty yards from their hiding place.

When they had eaten, Toby tiptoed away to a nearby tree to relieve himself. Coming back he heard shouting, so close that it startled him, followed by the sharp buzz of an engine. Jim White, crouching down, signalled frantically. The boy scrambled into the shelter of the silo. Jim clamped Ranger's mouth shut, then motioned to Toby to take hold of the dog. His hands free, he slipped his crossbow off his back and loaded it.

Long minutes passed. Suddenly, two children, a boy and a girl, burst out of the concealing bushes and sprinted up the path from the south. They ran wildly, in evident terror, their bodies flung desperately forward, their young muscles strained to the limit. About ten years old, and not visibly mutants, the children were dressed in rough jeans and jackets; they might have been farm children, pursued by some wild animal. Neither cried out nor spoke, but as they came opposite the silo they hesitated for a moment, casting a quick look at the structure, as if they might seek shelter there. Then, with one impulse, they turned away off the path and disappeared in the thick bush that stretched toward a nearby stand of cedars.

They were out of sight, but those childish faces, sick with pure terror, stayed in Toby's mind. He started to say something to Jim White, but at that instant two motorcycles roared up the path. Two women rode the clumsy vehicles, the smears of their bright red lipstick visible even from a distance, their long, braided hair swinging out from beneath brown berets. They were dressed in black leather jackets and boots, and they had sleek, high-powered rifles strapped to their shoulders. The weapons were more deadly and efficient-looking than any the boy had seen before.

Opposite the silo, they hesitated, and finally stopped. They stood there, leaning on their powerful machines, kicking at the rough track with shiny boots. Then, having exchanged a few words, they nodded, and seemed about to investigate the silo, swinging their bikes around toward the crumpling concrete

Jim White shifted his big shoulders, clutched tight at his crossbow; Toby held Ranger with white-knuckled fingers.

At that moment, though, the women changed their minds. They turned, cutting back north on the track, pointing their vehicles toward the screening cedar stand. Slowly, they bumped away, disappearing among the trees, the irregular roars of the engines shaking the lacy branches like a foul wind.

Jim White put down his crossbow and mopped his sweating brow. Toby looked at him questioning-ly, but the man only grunted, all the while eyeing

Toby closely, as if he were trying to make up his mind what to say.

"The children will escape," he said finally, leaning back against the bunker. "I'm pretty sure of that. They had good reason to be terrified, though. I've seen those women before."

He paused for a moment, cast a sharp look at Toby. "I don't like this at all. It means there are going to be more sacrifices. And the bikers are not the worst of it. The worst of it is who's using some of these bikers: a man named Azmud. Those women are known as Azmud's collectors."

Toby started to speak — he had a thousand questions — but Jim White pushed the questions away with a gesture. The steady drone of engines sounded in the distance.

"Not now. I can't tell you anything. You'll learn for yourself soon enough. Right now we have to rest. You hear those engines? There won't be much sleep for us tonight. So just settle down and don't fret about things that you can't do anything about."

They lay in the bunker until the sun had gone down and the woods were swallowed up by thick darkness. Then they went forward, Jim leading the way unerringly, as if he were following a magical thread through the black tangle of underbrush and wind-stirred trees.

They marched grimly for a while, then Jim White called a halt. Toby could still hear the incessant engines, but now a new sound was audible: a low murmur of voices, a solemn chanting that seemed to rise out of the forest nearby. The melody floated down to them, slithering and turning with a serpentine beauty and strangeness. The boy listened, fascinated. His fingertips touched the bare tree trunk beside him. He became aware of a thin drift of smoke, faint but acrid, settling down on the thicket where he stood.

Toby could contain himself no longer. "What is this, Jim? Where are we?" he whispered, a little too loudly, for the black man seized his arm suddenly in a fierce grip.

"*Silence, boy*!" he whispered with ferocity. He shoved Toby down against the tree trunk. "Just be quiet until I tell you."

They crouched together in the shadows. The slow drone of chanting continued. Toby's excitement, his hurt at being rebuffed, gave way to a state of suspension in which he drifted along with the music, lulled half asleep as the faint acrid odour persisted and seemed to dull his senses. He gazed up dreamily at the winking stars.

Then, all of a sudden, Jim White was shaking him, propelling him back into consciousness. How much time had passed he did not know, but the music had stopped, though the chanting and murmuring still echoed faintly in the boy's mind.

"It's time to go," Jim said.

They moved on again through the darkness, emerged from a rough circle of hedges, and stood in an open space beside a high fence. In the silvery starlight the posts made a phalanx of shadows.

They stepped across a fallen post at a place where the fence had collapsed. The boy looked up. Stone figures rose in the moonlight, giant forms looming out of the shrubbery.

*Dinosaurs*, the boy thought.

Jim White led Toby along a curving path. As he walked, he pointed up at the huge-bodied beasts. Some of these had long curving necks and great tails; others stretched their horned heads, or bore razorback fins like the edges of giant scallop shells.

A few of the figures were decorated, smeared over with bright paint; others had been slung round with crude garlands, bare wreaths blown and shredded by the early spring winds. But what was strangest of all to Toby was that, though the gates and some of the walls around the park had been smashed down, the figures themselves were nearly all whole; here and there missing a part, but mostly intact.

"Where are we, Jim?" Toby asked with a wave of his hand toward the broken gates, the great barrier, and the thrusting stone heads. "Are these dinosaurs? The teacher told us about them once, but I didn't know there were statues of them. I never thought I'd see them as big as life. And none of them are busted up."

"You're right. These are dinosaurs, the old creatures of the earth." Jim nodded. "There's a name for them — misused by men: Leviathan. The mutants come here, and some of their biker friends. Azmud has been here, too. I can sense his presence."

"Azmud?"

Jim White pulled the boy down in the shrubbery. "Take a good look at that place," he said. "You heard the voices, the ceremony. You know what the mutants do there? They perform sacrifices to those idols. They even claim to be connected with the old reptiles. You know what *lineage* is, boy?" Jim smiled grimly. "Genetic inheritance, some would call it. The mutants claim their genes got mixed up with reptile genes that some scientists activated in the twenty-first century. They reject what's human in them, just because they can do things ordinary humans can't. They can read minds and move objects, things like that. They sacrifice ordinary humans to their master, to their idols. They claim it gives them power. They feed on power — like Satan himself. And Azmud is the worst of them."

Toby stared at him. "Is Azmud a mutant, then?"

Jim laughed bitterly. "Azmud was once a great leader: a priest and preacher. That was after the time of troubles, after the collapse of everything. But his power corrupted him. And I was sent to deal with him, to cast him down. I failed in my mission then, because I was too confident of my power. By that time he'd changed — and made himself almost invulnerable. So he eluded me, and he mocked me. And I went into the desert and disciplined myself. I became stronger. And now I'm ready to challenge him. Because he's got spiritual power, he thinks he's something like a king, or a god. But he has a master, too, and his is the worst of all. His master is —"

Jim caught himself in mid-sentence. "But I can't tell you any more. It isn't permitted me. Some day the truth may dawn on you. Just remember that when human misery is at its worst and the world gets to seem hopeless, new forces can rise up and change things. It's then you can catch a glimpse of what's hidden; it's then that good and evil, the high powers, put on human faces."

As he spoke these words, Jim White gave Toby a look that he never in his life forgot. It was a sad look, distant yet warm, a look full of knowledge and power, one that seemed to come from somewhere far beyond the binding necessities, the stark limitations of the everyday, fearful world that surrounded them.

They moved on, and just beyond the enclosure, they found the great highway. They hid their packs among the trees and stood in the shadows, watching the cars and trucks roar past on the nearby road. Behind them, above the trees and the high barrier, rose the heads of the great statues, lit up from time to time by the flash of a quick headlight beam as some enormous vehicle thundered past them.

"Where are all those cars going?" Toby asked, listening to the sharp whine of the engines. He had never seen anything remotely like it.

Jim White laughed softly in the darkness. "Nowhere," he chuckled. "That highway only stretches for thirty miles or so in a pretty straight line. It's all that's left of the old roads that used to connect everything to everything. It's a terrible road, full of potholes and ditches, but the bikers and some others that have working vehicles still like to race here. They have guns, too, and get into killing each other about it. We have to cross over fast before sun-up. This place isn't healthy for the likes of us."

Jim led the way back to where they had stowed their packs. The dog moved in and out of the dark shrubbery. The roar of the engines followed them. Through the trees, lights darted, as if the ancient highway were signalling them. Toby followed Jim, then stood gaping, first at the great road, and then at the dinosaur park.

The air smelled of gas fumes mingled with a sweeter odour — it might have been cooked flesh.

Toby's heart sank; his throat went dry and he could ask no more questions. The papers in his father's care had revealed to him some of the past horrors of their world, but now he had experienced something more. He had begun to understand the abasement of everything, the sacrilege. The bikers were not even the worst of it. Their ruined world had adopted evil ways, evil worship. That was what his father and the other Old Believers had sought to atone for by carrying out the laws of their ancestors, by keeping the old customs, by burying the dead. But now his father was helpless, and it was up to Toby, with Jim White's help, to bring back the treasure that might save him.

The boy called softly and Ranger ran over and crouched beside him. Toby clung to the dog's neck, praying that the bikers had not returned to find his father.

# CHAPTER EIGHT

They rested, and, at the first light of dawn, crossed the great highway.

As they scrambled out of the thick bush and sprinted toward the trees on the opposite side, curls of smoke twisted up from a wrecked car lying shattered in among the pines and the boulders. No vehicles passed at that moment, but Toby whistled softly, just to keep Ranger close. He had caught one brief glimpse of a body stretched out on the margin of the road, a fire-blackened corpse jackknifed against a snapped-off highway sign.

Breathing hard, they ducked in among the trees and sprawled down. Toby's sleep-sodden mind echoed with gunfire and the shrill whine of engines; Jim noticed his anxiety, and reached out and patted his shoulder.

"Take it easy, boy," Jim White smiled. "We're in daylight nightmare country now, and you'll have to be strong. And we'll have to keep Ranger on this rope I've got. There shouldn't be many travellers, but we can't take the main path without inviting trouble."

They moved cautiously along a low hillside, then up through the trees. Rotting leaves, released by the spring thaw, made soft patches underfoot. The woods, not yet thick with full growth, seemed to resonate quietly. The land was pleasant and gently rolling; a light mist drifted up and vanished as the sun rose higher.

For some hours, Toby was aware of the low drone of the cars on the highway behind them, but toward noon these sounds faded and he heard, not far away, the rushing of water, and from all around them the song of the spring birds.

They ate lunch on a sunny rock ledge overlooking a point where the trail divided; there were two narrow valleys, one running east-west with the main path, the other cutting off toward the south.

"If you follow that gap to the west," Jim White told the boy as they shared food from the packs, "eventually you get to Apple Valley. It's a place you may go some time. There are no bikers there now; the law has come back. Life is good there, if you're willing to work. But south of here, where your relative John Wilson lives, things are a little different."

He paused and fed the dog some cheese from his hand.

"You know everything about this land, don't you, Jim?" the boy said.

"I've been travelling here for a long time," the man told him, rising to his full height. "Right now we've got to head south; there's no point in wasting time here."

Toby stood up. He was noticing, as if in a new way, the scroll of lines on the other's weathered face. Jim White suddenly seemed very old, but a quickness animated his whole body. Now Toby looked at him questioningly, as if it were finally time for an explanation.

"You have to trust me a little longer," Jim said. "We may not get exactly what you expect at Wilson's place. But there's a reason for us to go there."

"Do you mean Dad may not get his money?"

"No more right now. Just remember, from now on, do what I tell you and don't stop to question. Your life may depend on it."

Toby wanted to argue, to question him even more, but the big man strode away, and the boy could only shrug his shoulders and follow, straining to keep hold of the dog, who seemed suddenly to be on a hot scent.

Walking south, they followed a faint track leading up and over a low rise; then the trees closed in, woods of birch and maple, interrupted here and there by small sunny clearings. They moved single-file on the trail, Jim's top hat lifting and bouncing as it brushed against the low, light-leafed branches. The boy found himself thinking of his father, of the old man waiting back at the homestead in a darkness that Toby must somehow disperse.

As they trudged on, and Jim's manner grew more sombre, the boy felt isolated and alone. He needed reassurance, explanations, some good news, but Jim White ignored him.

Their trail wound at last down through a stand of white and yellow birch trees, then into the open, where Toby caught a glimpse of a rough road, and of fields spreading out across a wide valley. There was no sign of a house, and no sound except the tramp of their boots, Ranger's scuffling movements, and the chattering of the birds in the thickets nearby.

When at last they stopped, Jim White slipped off his pack and split up their supplies, leaving a cache under a shelf of flat stones beside a huge mossy boulder. He cut some trail marks as they pushed ahead. They came out cautiously on the road, the sunlight dazzling after their trek through the shadow-dappled woodlands.

Along the valley they trudged. Around them the fields lay unkempt, their deep furrows rigid and hard, tufted over with rough grass. Everywhere snake fences ran, some with supporting posts that had gone askew, in many places the cedar logs caved in or missing. Small stands of thickly clustered pines, copses spilling out of their former boundaries, grew in the near fields.

A few miles farther along, Toby stopped, and looked questioningly at Jim. Just ahead he saw something else, something puzzling. Two, three, seven scarecrow-like figures rose in stark outline above the low, tangled grass. Lanky figures, strapped to stout poles, they were dressed in black coats and straw hats that tilted down low on their faces. Their clothing looked shabby and ragged, as if it had been torn at by angry hands. The scarecrow arms were stretched out crosswise, and Toby saw a flash of white at a few of the black sleeves. The boy scrambled over a snake fence and began walking across the field toward the nearest figure. Ranger ran in circles, barking.

"Hold on," Jim White cautioned. The boy stopped and Jim caught him up. His expression was grim. "Let's go check it out together," he said quietly.

They crossed a patch of soggy field, where the wild grass was dotted with small stones and bird droppings.

A slight breeze stirred the stubble and lifted the black sleeve of the figure right in front of them. The scarecrow seemed to huddle into itself, its hat concealing the false face, its baggy suit flapping a little on the rough wooden post. A large carrion crow sat on a boulder nearby, nodding and croaking quietly. It did not fly away as they approached.

Jim White walked slowly up to the scarecrow figure. Gently, he plucked out a few wisps of straw that dribbled through a gash in the coat. Then with quick fingers he made the sign of the cross in the air, reached up, and pushed away the straw hat.

Toby cried out and stepped back. He saw that the figure had been constructed from a human corpse.

Hollow-eyed and vacant, a skull grinned at them. Tiny black ants crawled in and out of the eye sockets. Someone had recently skewered a plump rat and placed it carefully, like an offering, in the open jaws.

Jim White said something quickly in a language the boy did not understand. He lifted the rat carefully from its place and flung it away. The crow leapt up from its boulder and fluttered away across the field, crying out as it flew.

Toby swallowed hard. Perhaps it was a trick of the light, or because the boy had shut his eyes on the horror, but for an instant it seemed as if the rat had simply vanished in the air.

Toby could not utter a sound, but his hands and shoulders moved as if shaping a question. Whining pitifully, Ranger had begun to circle the skeleton.

"Listen to me, boy," Jim White told him, an almost vicious strength in his voice. "Don't think about this thing. Don't let it work on your mind. Our troubles begin right this minute and we've got to be very careful. Just follow me, do what I say, and above all, don't let it work on your mind."

Jim turned away. He strode across the hard furrows and slipped through a gap in the snake fence. As Jim rejoined the road, Toby followed him, still aware of each grim, hanging figure, but averting his eyes as they passed them, one by one. He kept looking at the big man, who, all the while, muttered strange words and made quick, odd signs in the air like a conjuror.

For a while they tramped along the rough, bare road. When they came to a crossroads, Jim took the left-hand path. Through a muddy field they went, then up a small rise toward a tall plantation, a thick stand of pines that concealed the shape of the land beyond, Toby glanced over his shoulder; the black figures were barely visible, mere specks in the distant sunlit fields. The boy felt sick. Slipping into the shelter of the trees, he threw himself down beside Jim on a thick carpet of needles.

Jim White breathed heavily as he swept off his top hat and slowly mopped at his brow with the red bandanna he had loosened from his neck. He looked at Toby with a grim, crinkled smile, unstrapped his crossbow, and sat there toying with the mechanism while he spoke to the boy in a low voice.

"We'll cut through these woods and get in sight of the house. I have a good idea what's going on there, but we need to work out our plan of attack."

Toby, still frightened by what he had seen in the fields, could hardly contain himself "What do you mean, *our plan of attack*? What's happening here, Jim? Why can't we just get the money from Mr. Wilson and clear out? This is a horrible place. Can't we just ask for what's owed Father and get away before the bikers who did those things get back? They've got to be crazy, completely crazy, the people who did that."

He waved desperately at the fields that stretched out, partially visible, behind them, offering up their grisly burdens in the calm sunlight.

Jim leaned forward. "Now just a minute, boy. This is no time to lose your good sense. I have to explain something. I can't tell you everything, but there are a few things you must know. First, there ain't no money here for your father. All right now, don't put on that long face. I knew all the time there was none."

"But why ...?"

"I know, you think without the money the trip is wasted — that we can't help your father — but that isn't true. Just do what I say and I think we can help the old man somehow."

Very slowly and carefully, Jim White took out of his backpack the two flasks, one containing the venom, and the other the entrails of the rattlesnake, and set them down side by side next to the crossbow.

"I told you, I travel a lot in these parts. I also told you I had a dream and it came to me that I should turn up at your farm. That's because I knew about Azmud."

"What did you know about Azmud?"

"That he was the one who killed Wilson, who killed those poor folk in the field. The one who's been looting the farm. Nobody else could handle Azmud, but I might be able to — with your help. As I told you, I've been waiting to tackle him for a good long time."

"But if there's no money left, why are we here at all? I don't understand."

"I said there was no money, boy. But there is a treasure."

Toby's eyes widened in astonishment. Wilson dead, and no money for his father? But Jim White smiled grimly, and began unscrewing the cap of the flask containing the venom.

"You see, all those poor murdered men in the fields had one thing in common: they wanted to be bridegrooms. Don't look so astonished — just hand me one of those arrows and listen carefully to what I say. If everything goes right, you can be on your way back to your father before sunset."

With great care, Jim White dipped the arrows, one by one, into the flask of venom.

"To cure a person's blindness is sometimes easier than to make him want to see," he said, without looking at the boy. "The entrails in that flask can cure Talby. Together with this venom, they can also help defeat Azmud. You can take that flask and go home to your father, or you can trust it to me for a little while, and go against Azmud. The choice is up to you."

Toby felt Jim's profound gaze encompass him, as if it were seeking out his soul. From childhood everything had been hard; sometimes he had not known what could possibly lie on the very next turn of the path; often he had felt himself trapped and defeated. But now, watching the sunlight glitter high up in the pine branches, feeling the strength of the man's presence beside him, the boy knew, inchoately, but with a blinding clarity, that everything he had experienced before had been by way of preparation for this moment. And he remembered that his father had once told him that a single thought, a clear wish, or the act of an instant, could mean the difference between heaven and hell.

"Well, boy," Jim White said sharply. "Don't sit there gawking. Do we work together or not?"

Toby picked up the flask containing the entrails of the snake he had killed and handed it to Jim.

"But what about Ranger?" he asked quickly, rubbing his hands on the Labrador's black silky coat. "I don't want to leave him behind."

Jim smiled. "I reckon he can help, then. Just hold him tight on the rope."

# CHAPTER NINE

Minutes later, they were moving quietly through the pine-carpeted wood. Jim White, his crossbow at the ready, led the way. The boy followed, hushing the dog with soft patter, gazing nervously back as the green depths closed in around them. They had gone only about fifty paces when Jim White raised his hand.

"Crouch down now, and follow me closely," he told the boy in a fierce whisper.

The high, screening branches gave way; an open space loomed, full of sunlight. Over Jim's shoulder Toby saw a green hillside sloping down, a house rising up in a hollow. The sweet scent of the pines soothed his anxious mind a little.

They had stopped at the edge of the plantation and were gazing out across the rolling meadow. Directly before them stood a house: a big sprawling farmhouse of weathered brick, with high, steep-pitched roofs, tall, narrow windows, and decorations of white carved gingerbread

They looked across at what seemed to be the kitchen entrance, fronted by a white wooden porch, with steps leading down to the muddy front yard. At the foot of the porch steps, side by side, sat two gleaming motorcycles, and one of them, a Harley, all bright red and covered with chrome, was the largest Toby had ever seen. "He's here, all right," Jim White whispered hoarsely. "Now we just have to wait for the right moment."

They settled down quietly in their hiding place at the edge of the trees. A thousand disturbing questions came to Toby's mind, yet staring intently at the scene before him, he thought to himself what a fine house it was down there in the hollow, what a fine life must have gone on there once. Why then, did the very air around them seem tense and fearful and full of danger? Why did the sunlight appear so deceptive, and why did the homely beauty of the old farmstead seem both illusory and unstable?

Toby sighed, closed his eyes, and waited. He yawned, dozed a little, but was brought back to reality by a sharp jab in the ribs. Jim White gripped his arm.

The door of the farmhouse swung open. A burly man with short, clipped hair, and wearing a black leather jacket, strolled out. Slung over the man's right shoulder was an automatic rifle. Compact, muscular, and dangerous-looking, he meandered along, swishing the small whip he carried in his right hand, and blinking in the sunlight as if he had been in the dark for a long time.

He peered up and down the length of the hollow, then eased his way to the bottom of the steps. From the smaller motorcycle, a Kawasaki, he lifted a gleaming gold helmet, pulled it on, thrust the whip in his belt, and kicked the engine to life.

The roar shook the pines, booming noise rattled the branches. The rider bumped away across the pitted yard and disappeared beyond a screening row of old hedges. They could hear the engine droning away in the distance.

Jim White turned to the boy and held up one finger. "One gone."

Once again, they settled down in their hiding place, watching. No sound, nothing visible, gave evidence of life within the house. The sun moved slowly across the sky. Jim White pulled a few crusts of bread from his pack and offered them to the boy.

Toby's shoulders and arms began to ache. He shifted his position uneasily, feeling tense and uncertain. He had trusted Jim, followed his every instruction; he half-believed they might succeed, that they might return in good time to help his father. At the same time, he wondered about many things. Why was

Jim White determined to help him and his father? What were they waiting for? Who might come out of the house?

Jim White had closed his eyes as if to rest "I have to ask you," the boy burst out suddenly. "Why did you lie to my father? Why did you let him think you were related to us?"

The boy felt the man move beside him, as if he were tightening his muscles, or stretching a little underneath the pine boughs.

"Would your father have let you come with me, you think, if he had known that I'm black? That he was talking to old Top Hat, the crazy man of the woods? Get some sense, boy!"

Toby licked his lips. He remembered his father's account of his consoling dream — the angel all shining and golden. He was puzzled. Ranger stirred at his side and the boy embraced him. Then he settled back, still bursting with questions, though he said nothing.

They kept watch.

As the sun moved, the grass seemed to catch fire, and a fierce light blazoned at the high windows of the house. The deep gloom that lay beyond the wide-open barn doors was given form by a few criss-crossing gold bars of light.

They waited, listening to the wind and watching clouds and shadows, when all at once a clear music sounded, the low tuneful sound of a single instrument, a flute perhaps, playing somewhere in the barn's gold-stirred darkness.

"That's it!" Jim White murmured grimly. He rubbed his eyes and rolled over, reaching for the cross-bow he had set down beside him. "Now listen careful-ly to me," he told Toby, and he began to unfold his instructions in short, whispered sentences.

The boy listened to his words and to the faint soothing music beyond, at the same time keeping watch on the barn door. After a while something bright stirred there, in the mouth of the darkness, and the boy saw the flash of a white cloth.

Then the door of the house suddenly opened and a girl emerged — a slender, striking girl — carrying a large jug and a round loaf of bread. She made her way carefully down the steps, descending with slow grace, almost as if she were sleepwalking.

Toby held his breath. She was the most beautiful girl he had ever seen. Jim White was silent, as if he were also watching her.

The girl wore a long, green, cotton dress with short sleeves and little puffed shoulders. She was barefoot, and her dress seemed a little tattered and faded, though brushed with soft pink as with the dust of wild roses. When she sprang with a coltish grace across the barn-yard, her dark hair flowing out behind her, it seemed to

Toby as if, in the clear air, she had suddenly awakened from a dream.

Approaching the barn she slowed her pace, her shoulders hunched a bit, and she hesitated. Toby could not take his eyes from her.

"Wilson's daughter, Sarah," Jim White said in a whisper. "Those murdered ones — back there in the field — they all wanted to marry her. There was no hope for them — Azmud saw to that — but maybe you'll have a chance."

Toby turned to Jim and saw his faint, grim smile; then he reached across to take the small metal flask that Jim held out in his tight-knuckled fist.

"Remember: have courage, and do just as I've told you. If you get clear, don't look back," Jim White said.

While Jim spoke, the boy was aware of the young girl, her white arms flashing in the sunlight as she carried the bread and the drink up to the big, open doors of the barn. She set the food and water down there, on the verge of the shadows, then stepped back and waited, while the flute went on sounding across the yard.

The music quickened. The girl listened for a while, and then, to the boy's amazement, she began to dance.

It was a slow, stately dance, and Sarah moved her body gently, seductively, turning and swaying with white, upraised arms. Three times around the food and drink she danced, tossing her head back, her whole body blossoming in the music.

Toby had never seen anything like it. He caught his breath; it was as if a spear had been thrust in the pit of his stomach.

This was what he had always thought of as "sin," something his father had spoken of in a hard sober way: the temptation of the flesh. Yet, watching the girl, he felt his spirits soar; he wanted to rise up on the tips of his toes and dance with her forever in the sunlight. At the same time, he was desperately anxious to say something to Jim, to break the spell of the music, but his mouth had gone dry, and he could barely swallow. His heart beat faster, and the palms of his hands began to sweat.

At last, without warning, the music stopped. The girl stood facing the barn doors, then slowly bent down, almost as if she were bowing.

A figure appeared from the shadows within the barn. A very tall man, as it seemed, a long spidery man in a white cotton suit, with silver-blond hair and blank blue eyes, and long stretching fingers that looked as if the nails curved out into claws. A small hollow tube at his belt might have been a flute.

Jim White's grip tightened on the boy's arm. "It's Azmud," he said in a fierce whisper. "Get ready."

The figure from the barn took a few steps forward, so that he stood between the spread out offerings and the girl, who seemed to have crumpled up, squatting down there on the bare turf. As he moved, Azmud's body quivered all over: it made the boy think of an insect. His awe at the sight of the apparition gave way to anger: what right did *he* have to control *her*, to make her dance that way, to make her carry his food?

"Now!" Jim White said, patting Toby smartly on the shoulder. The boy climbed to his feet and stepped out of the trees. The dog, released from the rope, and overjoyed at his freedom, ran some paces ahead.

Azmud looked up; his left hand slid to his belt. The girl turned and stared hard at Toby, the palms of her hands spread out flat on the grass.

Toby's pace faltered. The dog, which had prowled down the hill, scampered back. The boy sensed Ranger's terror; he pressed his thumb hard against the open top of the flask at his side. It was strapped loosely to his belt, and he knew it would come away quickly when he yanked at it.

*"You mustn't look down at the flask,"* Jim had told him. *"And above all, don't look back up the hill. Just keep on talking. It doesn't matter if you're nervous. He'll expect you to be nervous. Anybody would be, talking to him. But, you can do it, boy. I know you can do it."*

Toby took a deep breath and walked forward. The dog crouched beside him, whining gently. He must not walk directly down toward Azmud, Jim had told him.

He must veer off a little, toward the left side of the house, then perhaps Azmud would step over toward him, away from the place where the girl crouched.

The boy tried to keep this in mind, but as he moved forward, step by step, the figure of Azmud seemed to rise up and take possession of the space around him. The man stood immobile, simply watching; only his head turned, almost imperceptibly, toward the boy. Yet Toby felt as if each of his steps met a new weight of air; a heaviness clogging the clear space between them seemed to harness his body. He knew he could not run, or move quickly at all. A terrible fear, the fear of his own helplessness, oppressed him. He felt the girl's gaze, on his face, on his hands.

"Well, what have we here? A new suitor?"

Azmud spoke slowly, in a soft, high-pitched voice. The boy struggled forward. The dog slunk away. The tall man looked down at him with a faint smile; the slits of his eyes flashed a bright, speckled blue; his fingernails gleamed as he slipped the long flute-like tube from his belt. Toby felt a weight like stone on his chest. He wanted to run but he could not; nor could he force himself forward.

From about thirty feet away, he saw everything: the pain in the girl's face, and the man's bloodless stare. And he saw the drained, white cast of his flesh, the lustreless white hair, and the eyes with their flecked blue. Azmud was one of the pale ones: an albino, a mutant!

As if sensing the boy's recognition and terror, the man laughed. He looked quite blithe, almost handsome. At that moment the girl gave a brief, stifled cry. Azmud turned quickly and hissed the word "silence." The girl toppled down in her place.

In that instant, Toby could breathe. He stepped sideways, back toward the house, touched the flask at his belt with his right hand.

"Water," he cried out. His choked voice surprised him. "I need water."

Azmud came toward him. His long limbs seemed to float in the air, and his white clothing gleamed in the sunlight. With a sharp, stiff-armed gesture, he raised the small tube to his lips.

Toby saw that it was a kind of blow gun, pointing straight at him. Behind Azmud the barn, as if held on a tether to the earth, rose and settled; the man's face seemed to melt — darkness closed in on the boy. Yet he mustn't go under!

Then a voice boomed down the hillside. "THE ANGEL OF DEATH HAS COME FOR YOU, AZMUD!"

A soft twang filled the air. The man in white straightened up and took two twirling steps, as if dancing.

Toby sprang forward and flung the contents of the flask in his face.

Azmud fell backwards, and propped himself up on one skinny arm. One feathered bolt had struck his chest, and he wriggled like a spider turned over, his thin body shaking, his head twitching wildly. He screamed, a high-pitched wild shriek, and the boy saw his face swell and bloat, the features dissolving in a maggoty whiteness.

Toby flung himself across the yard, toward the girl. At that moment Jim White, like a great agile cat, came bounding up beside him. Jim's eyes blazed, his breath came in gasps; with a quick shove he sent Toby sprawling back toward the house, then swept up the girl in his arms, shouting commands as he ran past the boy toward the great gleaming red Harley that sat parked at the foot of the steps.

"Move it, for God's sake. Get out of here, quick!"

Toby saw Azmud crawling awkwardly on his hands and knees toward the barn. A white film, like a faint spray of mist, seemed to enfold each deliberate motion of the man's body. The boy hesitated, half-paralysed by the sight of the insect-like beat of the arms and legs, and by the incessant shrieking that echoed between house and barn, filling up the whole space of the yard.

The sharp roar of the motorcycle stirred him into action. He dragged himself up. Jim White had started the engine and flung the girl down into the passenger seat, and he held her there now, shouting at the boy and beckoning.

"Good work, boy!" He pulled Toby toward the front of the cycle, then reached out and thrust a small flask into the boy's pocket. "The medicine for your father. Make sure you get it to him!" Jim White hugged Toby quickly, murmuring a few words that the boy did not understand, then with a cry, he sprang away after Azmud, who was just vanishing into the darkness of the barn.

The boy turned, laid hold of the handlebars of the cycle, and, feeling the girl's arms come around him, crouched forward, working throttle and clutch. The great engine roared and the handlebars shook. Its vibrations made his body tremble, and the girl's arms clasped him tighter; her head leaned down on his shoulder. Underneath him, up through his buttocks and spine, Toby felt the powerful, irregular throbbing of the machine.

# CHAPTER TEN

Only a few times in his life had Toby been on a bike. Mr. Koenich, his teacher, kept one at school and sometimes allowed the older students to ride it. Toby, everyone said, was a natural. That was a small rig, though, a Honda. Now the boy looked down at the Harley, and to his relief saw that he recognized a few things on this very different vehicle: the tachometer and the clutch lever, the front-brake grip, the dip switch, the kill button. He gritted his teeth, half-closed his eyes, and stretched himself to his full length. Then he put the monster in gear.

Smoothly, he worked the clutch, twisting the throttle with his right hand, and firming his grip on the handlebar as the engine roared violently beneath him.

They shook and swayed, bumping and throbbing slowly across the rutted farmyard.

The driveway curved away from the house, down an incline, past a few scraggly poplars to the wide-open gate. Toby hung on, not daring to look back, fearful of the power of the engine, which fired continuous and shattering bursts, as if shells were exploding beneath them. He kept opening the throttle, almost furtively, and the engine responded with sharp, nervous surges, which shook the steel frame and sent a wayward tremor along the boy's haunches and thighs.

With an effort, he controlled the Harley, but didn't dare ride faster than a jogging pace. Once through the gate he took the road that circled back around the pine woods.

They had not gone a mile, bumping along, moving quite slowly, when Ranger burst out of the trees and, putting on speed, coasted past them, barking and tossing his head as the pebbles and dust sprayed around him.

"Good boy," shouted Toby, glad that his pace was slow enough that Ranger could keep up.

With the Harley under control, Toby craned round and tried to speak to the girl. He could glimpse only her forehead, cream-white, and the curve of her nose, then a soft fringe of dark hair. Her white arms still encircled his waist, long fingers locked in a tight grip. When he shouted, she responded, her chin digging into his shoulder, but her words drifted off in the harsh roar.

The girl clung to him, yet Toby wondered: when they stopped at the end of the road and he asked her to go on with him, would she simply turn back? Would she run away?

In his mind, the boy saw Jim White locked in a hand-to-hand struggle with Azmud. Jim was strong, but the evil one, though transfixed by a bolt from the crossbow and scorched by the venom, might still gather new strength. Maybe it was impossible to destroy him. Maybe the mutant would pursue them later, all the way back to the homestead.

To the homestead! Toby felt his resolve sharpen. They rode past field after field. He kept his eyes fixed on the road, skirting potholes, his confidence rising as he steered the great machine. Leaning right and left, he heard the engine smooth out. Its power flowed up through his body; he watched the speedometer rise.

Then, without warning, the girl struck his back and at the same time cried out, her words eaten up by the roaring machine. He braked a little; her fingers clawed at his shoulder. They coasted. And he gazed down the road where she pointed.

At the crossroads, just two fields ahead, a dark figure crouched. Sunlight spilled over the stranger's shoulder, outlining man and bike, and the rifle slung over his back.

The boy slowed even more, thinking fast, trying to keep his balance.

"That's Brack!" the girl cried in his ear, pounding on Toby's shoulder with one small fist. "He's waiting there to kill us!"

Toby tightened his grip on the bars; his whole body stiffened, and he screwed his eyes half-shut, as if by sheer willpower he could propel his machine past their enemy.

But the other bike, too, had started moving. The man called Brack roared straight toward them, accelerating fast.

Toby was horrified. Were they going to meet head-on in the roadway?

Ranger raced up beside them, a dark blur streaking past the slow-moving machine at full speed. Toby gasped when he saw him: the dog was making straight for the oncoming Brack.

Brack saw the dog, but too late. Ranger leapt. His body hurled through the air, just brushing the man's sleeve, yelping as he spun away and landed on all fours in the roadside. Brack braked and swerved, skidding wildly. The machine tilted, then shot sideways, gathering gravel and dust. It roared straight for the ditch.

Toby stopped his machine and watched in horror as Brack's Kawasaki arced briefly, smashed through the fence, and crashed into the field. He heard the man's shrill cry, the ear-splitting whine of the engine. Sparks showered everywhere. The bike flamed. The dog came racing back. He stood by the wreck, barking furiously.

The boy accelerated the Harley and they rattled along slowly, as if in a trembling nightmare, past the fallen man, and past the crumpled and smouldering machine, the smashed fence, and the barking dog. Then Toby stopped the machine and sat for a few moments in a daze. Everything had happened so quickly.

The girl pounded on his shoulder. "For God's sake, let's get out of here!" she begged.

Ranger crawled through a gap in the fence and lounged on the road just ahead of them, wagging his tail nonchalantly and waiting. Toby got the machine in motion again. He roared past Ranger, and the dog followed, bounding along beside them, his nose pressed close to the road. Toby leaned forward, in a daze of shock and horror. The sun was about to slip down among the dark trees. Behind him, the girl was sobbing quietly.

They rode for another mile or two, and then Toby brought the machine to a rough stop. The engine went on idling.

Suddenly, Ranger started to bark. Something extraordinary was happening in the fields close beside them.

They had come upon the ghastly scarecrows, which hung as before, seven figures stretched on low posts, but different now, much darker despite the sunset light, each splayed out and controlled by a darkness that seemed to boil up from beneath the patched and comical clothing, the straw-packed sleeves.

Toby stared at the blurred, half-opaque figure hanging there above the ragged furrows. Was it his imagination, or could he really see the bleached white bones shining underneath the tilted hats, the shabby collars?

He shivered, and the light changed again. The girl pointed and started to say something.

The scarecrows moved and swayed. Beams of light from the dying sun, focused, it seemed, like a burning glass, struck them all at once and as they did so, smoke poured from gaping mouths, flames burst out, igniting the scarecrow coats. Bright wisps of straw drifted from hollow sleeves, winking away into the darkness.

"God help them," the girl whispered. One by one, the scarecrows had caught fire. In the nearest conflagration, in the heart of the flames, Toby could make out a skull, a frail shape of bones. When the post beneath it blackened, the skull toppled. The ghost of a cross hung in the air for a moment and then vanished.

The sun fell behind the shaggy trees. Seven beacons dimmed slowly in the near fields.

"They've escaped him now," the girl murmured.

Toby looked at her. He could not make sense of her words, nor of the strange sight he had just seen in the fields, but he was aware of the girl's beauty and of her strange, fixed expression as she stared past him into the darkening landscape.

As he gazed at her, Sarah leaned against him. He was held by the pain in her eyes, by the simple, fresh beauty of her face. She was shivering a little in her dress, its sleeves badly torn, its hem frayed and smudged. Her face had a faraway look. Was she perhaps a mad girl? Had she been swallowed up by a darkness like the one that now consumed the world around them? Like a beautiful sleepwalker, Sarah slipped off the machine and stood in the roadway. She looked around at the sombre fields, avoiding the boy's glance. Toby shut off the engine. He did not know whether he would be able to start it again, but it seemed to him not to matter.

He moved close to the girl and on an impulse took her in his arms; she looked up at him with a tear-streaked face. Tenderly, he kissed her cheeks and her forehead. She clung to him.

She was the first girl he had been alone with in his life. He was overwhelmed by her beauty, her deep sadness. He couldn't bear to speak, and though there was much he wanted to hear about her past, there were some things that he was already afraid to know.

It grew ever darker. All the light had drained away from the fields, but a few black posts still smouldered, and the air reeked of sour smoke.

Still they clung together as she spoke to him, in a low voice, almost in a whisper, and her questions seemed full of tenderness and deep concern.

"Who are you? Please tell me," she asked him. "And why did you come for me? I didn't think anyone else would come."

Toby told her his name, then glanced anxiously up the road. "We can't stop here. They may catch us. I didn't come to rescue you, but I'm glad I did. I'll explain later — I'll tell you everything I know. But we have to go now!"

He paused, but could not pull away, feeling her closeness, and struggling with his own mixed feelings: "You're so beautiful. I'm glad I found you," he blurted out.

She drew back, held him at arm's length, and gazed at him with her deep sad eyes. "I just wanted to die, but I couldn't," she whispered. "It was like a dream, only I was nothing, just a fragment, like a part of someone else's wish. It was a nightmare. I thought I would vanish, disappear from this earth ... and not even wake up. I couldn't wake up. Those boys who came to marry me ... they were lovely. I remember them, all of them. I would have married any of them. But they killed them! Azmud and Brack killed them all!"

"Don't worry," Toby told her. "All that's over now." But he wasn't confident, and glanced nervously back down the road.

"I understand things," she said. "I have a gift — you might call it a gift. And there's something I know, Toby."

She was the most vulnerable girl Toby had ever met, and yet he felt a strength in her, as if she were moved by some great impersonal force, a power of will that would never let her falter.

"What is it you know, Sarah?"

"I know that we're destined to share some part of life together, and I'm glad, because I can tell even now, when I hardly even know you, that you're very kind, and sweet, and that you need me as much as I needed you back there — as I need you now."

She pressed against him and they exchanged a long kiss. Toby, in rapture, struggled to break free of her spell.

At last he seized her hand and drew her over to the motorcycle. He pressed the starter, then revved up the engine. She climbed up behind and grabbed hold of him. They drove on steadily for a few miles, and only once did the boy glance back down the road, half expecting to see Jim White come after them. "*Don't wait for me anywhere along the way,*" Jim had told him. "*Get back to the homestead. Take the girl there as quickly as you can.*"

As they rode toward the deep woods, the chopper's powerful light beam began to take hold in the dusk. Toby's thoughts turned to his father. Even in the frenzy of the attack, Jim had remembered to pass him the flask with the snake's entrails. He knew it was in his pocket now, and he would guard it well; he would make sure it got to his father. But would that filthy stuff — the boiled innards of a snake — really help the old man? Jim White had seemed so confident that the contents of the little flask would work. "Trust me," he had told the boy. But now Jim was gone, and Toby's mind was overwhelmed by doubts. Even Sarah's anxious embrace, the sight of her slender fingers locked around his jacket, disturbed rather than reassured him. What would he tell his father when they returned? What would his father think of the girl, whose beauty the old man could not even get sight of?

They drove steadily forward; the road dwindled, the trees crowded round them, and the beam of the head-light revealed at last the gashed stump that marked the beginning of their trail through the woods.

Everything looked different at night, and the girl waited while Toby ran up among the trees to search for the trail sign and the small cache of supplies Jim White had left for him there.

The dog, who had no doubts, plunged on ahead through the darkness. Within a few minutes Toby had found what he sought. While Sarah stood by watching, he wheeled the machine down the road twenty paces, and with a good, running start toppled it down into the thickest part of the screening bushes. It was an outside chance, but if things worked out, they might just recover the valuable machine again.

When he walked back, anxious to lead the girl away at once to the woods, eager to start for home, he sensed her hesitation. In the darkness, she took his arm, pressing it and holding him there for a moment.

"We should have buried them," she said very quietly, and he knew that she was thinking of the men hung up in the fields, of her dead and desecrated suitors.

# CHAPTER ELEVEN

He led her up the trail through the trees, grateful for the silence that enfolded them. After a while, he took her hand to help her over a fallen birch trunk, and feeling how cold her fingers were, he rummaged through his backpack and found a thin slicker, which he draped around her shoulders. He pulled out a pair of his old, well-worn running shoes and she put them on. There was no moon and he could not see the girl clearly, but he was acutely aware of her presence beside him.

They struggled on for a while. Then on the edge of a clearing, the boy found a place, a kind of rough hollow space in the thicket. With his knife, he cut off some pine boughs and spread them out, then laid his coat across the boughs. He sat down on the coat and beckoned for the girl to sit beside him. After a while it got even colder, and they wrapped themselves up in the coat. Lying close, Toby felt the girl's warm body press against him. Her hair brushed his face.

He began to shiver, although not from the cold, and he was embarrassed.

"Here," she said, locking him in her arms. "Don't be shy."

He breathed in a light, pleasing scent. Was it the pine boughs or the scent of her white skin? Even in the thick darkness he sensed her wide eyes fixed on his; her fingers moved up his back and softly caressed his hair. It seemed to him that he had never felt so happy, so protected and loved, as at that moment. He drifted away into a vague dream of summer. Not once through the whole night did he sink into a deep sleep; rather, he swung gently from image to image, in touch with his body, yet drifting beyond it, drawn back by his sense of the girl there.

It seemed there was no sunrise, but simply a filtering down of grey light, accompanied by a sharp chill that forced Toby at last to his feet. He jumped up and down to warm himself while the girl watched him, smiling and yawning. Then she too got up and stood shivering, until he urged her to jump. For a while, they ran around the little clearing, playing a crazy kind of tag and throwing sticks for Ranger to retrieve from the tangled grass. Later, they found a stream nearby where they drank and washed.

Then they ate a few mouthfuls of bread and cheese, fed the dog on dry biscuits, and started on their way.

All day they tramped through the woods. A fine mist of rain fell. They ducked around low dripping branches, watched the track muddy up under foot, but pushed steadily on, stopping for a while where the path divided, one branch running west toward Apple Valley.

"Have you ever been there?" the boy asked in the assumed tones of an experienced traveller. They had spoken hardly at all, and Toby felt awkward. He'd got her to walk in front of him part of the way, just so he could watch her, but he could think of nothing to say. He knew he would have to tell her about his father, and somehow it embarrassed him. She seemed to have no concern about their destination.

"I've never been anywhere," she said quietly.

As they were about to start, she bent over to tighten the lace on the running shoes he had lent her and he saw the raw welts on her legs, stripe marks that cruelly disfigured the white skin. He turned away and pretended to play with the dog, but he felt something clutch at his soul. It was as if he had seen the rattlesnake rise once again from the murky water.

They started off, and he walked behind her, but kept his eyes fixed on the trail, more than ever aware of how all of her movements possessed him. He was ashamed of his own doubts, of his revulsion from what he imagined of her. What had Azmud done to the girl, what terrible things had she suffered? He cursed his own awkwardness, and pushed away the thoughts that came to him: things he remembered from the sly, obscene jokes of the schoolyard. He didn't want to think of the girl like that, seeing her walk there before him, moving lightly in her ragged, green, rose-patterned dress, just as if it were the fanciest party gown.

That night they slept less than a mile south of the great highway, tying up the dog and taking special care to conceal themselves within a thick press of cedars. It was damp; they had no fresh clothes, but they did not dare light a fire.

At first, they tried lying side by side in their clothes, underneath Toby's long coat, but the dampness came up; they tossed this way and that and felt miserable. After a while the girl took Toby's hand and made him sit up. She leaned close. In the dim light he saw how her cheeks glistened faintly with moisture.

"Toby," she said. His name sounded strange on her lips, and he swallowed and listened.

"You said there was a spare groundsheet in your pack. We didn't use it last night, but suppose ...," here she paused for one fleeting instant, "suppose we just wrapped that around us. I mean, if you ain't shy, we could take off these wet things."

The boy swallowed hard. He could not say a word; he felt his heart pounding wildly.

Slowly, she drew him up, seemingly taking his silence for assent. He stumbled over to the pack to get the ground sheet. In the darkness, he could sense that she was unhurriedly stripping down. Half-wrapping the stiff sheet around him, he tried to undress in his awkward cocoon, but it kept slipping down as he moved, and he heard her rippling laughter beside him.

"What on earth are you doing, Toby?"

He let the sheet fall, then pulled off his clothes and his boots and placed them on the branches of the tree, trying to avoid the dripping wet needles.

When he turned, she was near him, the sheet wrapped around her.

"I like you, Toby," she said in a low whisper. "I'm glad you came to find me."

They swung the sheet around them, fumbling and laughing in the darkness. At last they could lie down, and Toby felt the girl's slender body press against his. They lay touching; he was lifted up instantly into a warm swoon of tenderness. And after a while she led him to make love to her, gently urging him on, and responding with sweet passion. Toby felt all their motions punctuated by sharp moments of pleasure, each of which came to him freshly and yet with intimate familiarity, as if the hints and guesses of childhood were suddenly realized there with her.

He felt himself drift into sleep. The next thing he knew the girl, fully dressed, was bending over him, her face clear but anxious. A smear of orange light betokened sunrise; engines roared, surprisingly near.

"You said we had to cross the highway early," she reminded him.

He started to leap up, found himself naked, and recoiled. She laughed and tossed him a bundle of clothes. "I've packed everything," she said. "I'll wait with Ranger. You get dressed and come along."

Warily, they descended through the woods. All the while Toby was thinking, "She's my girl now. I love her." She fascinated him — her voice, her eyes, the way that she walked. Everything about her moved him; everything seemed unique and magical. He could not resist plucking a fresh white trillium from the cool shadows and setting it in her hair.

They tramped on and at last, coming out through a small pine forest, they made out the road, the old highway, pockmarked and slicked over with moisture. They hid there a while; a motorcycle passed, then another with a sidecar. They crept down to the margin, lying low in the scrub bush. From there they could not actually see very far down the highway, and they agreed to take a chance, to make a dash for it at the first sustained quietness. They waited, hearing nothing at all; Toby counted one, two, three, and they ran, Ranger scouting along ahead of them.

The paved road felt strange under foot. They giggled as they bounded across. It seemed a lark. But sharp voices cried out from not far away.

A red pickup truck sat parked on the margin, not two hundred feet from the point of their crossing. Two men crouched by the truck, changing a tire. At the sight of the boy and the girl they had shouted. Now they got up, calling loudly and waving their arms.

"Don't stop," Toby cried. "They think we're mutants."

The dog started barking. The girl ran ahead and ducked in among the trees. "Now which way?" she called out as Toby dashed up.

The boy hesitated. He was sure he had seen, far off to the left and high above the trees, the gleaming stone back of a beast from the dinosaur park.

"That way," he pointed. They plunged on, soaked through all at once in the thick bush. A shot rang out behind them, then another. They could hear the men's voices; their pursuers were swearing now, and firing at random. Toby kept glancing around, trying to get his bearings. After some time, and after the sound of voices and gunshots had ceased, they stopped to recover themselves.

"I think we've lost them," the girl said. She sat down on a stone and caught her breath. Toby called

Ranger, and made a leash for him with a coil of rope from his backpack.

Moving on, they found a faintly marked track and followed it some miles west, keeping a sharp watch ahead. Around them, the bushes filled up with light and the leaves, slicked with water, enclosed them like a luminous web. Behind them was silence, but ahead the woods thinned. Smoke drifted up toward the pink sky. Voices floated up from the trees.

Toby grabbed hold of the girl's sleeve and pointed. Sleek haunches of stone, the figures of dinosaurs, curved up out of the foliage.

"Do you hear that singing?" he asked. "It's coming from right over there, from the park. It's the worship! Jim White explained it. It seems some folks pray to those dinosaurs!"

At that moment, a wild chanting burst out; there was loud clapping of hands, a few moans and shouts. Flutes and drums sounded near, and smoke billowed up amid the frenzy of the music.

The colour drained from the girl's face. "I know that music," she murmured. "It's Leviathan's song. Azmud taught me it."

Toby remembered her dance by the barn; he thought of how she had clung to him, how she had moved by his side through the night. He thought of the marks he had seen on her legs and her thighs. He stood tense and hostile, staring down at the coiled grass.

"Toby, we've got to get out of here!" The girl shook him hard by the shoulders; he felt the rope squeezing his fingers as the dog strained and yelped.

"Come on," he said quietly as he took hold of her hand.

Striking out from the path, they struggled through thick bush and came out minutes later on the main trail. Some distance beyond the rutted track a zigzagging iron fence, horribly rusted, encircled the form of a dinosaur. They stared at the crouching lizard, its sloping, horned head and its curved tail part of another world, a different nightmare. Behind them, the music burst out, ecstatic, almost alluring in its intensity; the odour of cooked flesh assaulted their nostrils.

Neither spoke a word, but with a single impulse, they fled north up the trail.

"There's a silo a few miles ahead," Toby told her. "We can rest there."

By the time they sprawled down in the shelter of one of the ruined farm buildings, their jackets were stiff and damp with sweat.

Toby let the dog off his leash, then lay back, his head resting against the crumbling concrete. He was aware of the girl beside him, and watched her, a little furtively, as she wiped her damp forehead with the sleeve of her jacket. It was here, he remembered, that he had sat with Jim and peered out from the silo, and Jim had first uttered the name "Azmud."

He thought of the children, running in terror from Azmud's "collectors," and hoped they had escaped. Sarah had not been so lucky.

But Azmud was dead now, he prayed. Dead or powerless. And Sarah — at least on the surface — seemed to have forgotten her tormentors. Would she ever explain to Toby just what they had done to her? More than anything he wanted to help ease her suffering, to comfort her. Also — and the thought shamed him — he was curious. He imagined he would never be her equal until he knew what she knew.

# CHAPTER TWELVE

They pushed on, suddenly distant from each other, hardly speaking. The path skirted grim farmsteads and ruined buildings, and once or twice they had to hide, muzzling the dog, while armed travellers scouted past. After a while the distant droning of the highway faded, but there was a new sound far ahead: a thin, buzzing sound like a chainsaw.

Soon they came upon a place where sunlight glinted on metal. Couch grass and thistles thrust up between the wrecks of cars and cast-off tires; dandelions burst out among the twisted steel, and insects hummed everywhere. They had come to the place of despond, the vast dump that bordered the ancient river, where Toby had killed the snake and crossed with Jim on the car bridge.

Sarah gasped when she took in this grim landscape. It was clear they could not risk the path — the sounds from ahead were disconcerting — so they crept away into the heart of the rubble, keeping low, marking their progress by the gleam of the sunlight on the twisted steel, and taking sightings by means of the half-toppled tower of an old windmill that lay close to the car-bridge.

Voices and the roar of engines reverberated among the smashed barrels, the rusted-out chassis, the piles of battered hubcaps. A rat darted out of the mouth of a half-sunken drainpipe. Ranger yelped briefly and Toby and Sarah shrank away with a cry.

"We've got to be quiet," Toby whispered, his voice trembling. He hung tight to the dog's lead, and stroked him reassuringly. Ranger whined and scratched, his dark eyes alight with a brief excitement. The girl, too, seemed agitated.

The drainpipe angled away toward the bridge. Here the junk towered high and they crawled forward under its shelter, using the metal wall to conceal themselves. Toby clutched at the precious flask in his pocket, and eyed the damp holes and rusting metal. This was snake country, across the river from the place where he had killed the serpent.

Voices sounded from nearby, and the roar of motorcycle engines reverberated across the broken metal. The foul stench of the water had begun to choke them so that they hardly dared to breathe.

At last, through a low metal arch, bent and rusted, they caught sight of the black, sluggish river. Its surface glowed with a sinister light, as if green, melted glass had been poured in. They shifted place a little and gazed across at a narrow shelf of beach, clogged with bits of tar-paper and a few rotted railway ties, and slicked at the water's edge with a delicate green scum. The beach curved back toward the humped sodden cars, which formed a gleaming line across the river. That was the bridge Toby had already crossed and they saw at once that they could reach it by means of a short run along the beach. At the same time, they had to duck back beneath the drainpipe, pinned at that spot by what they saw on the other side of the river.

Six bikers roared around a huge blazing fire, stopping and starting, steering their bikes straight through the flames, bending quickly to pick up rag-stuffed bottles from sidecars placed nearby. They pitched these like home-made grenades into the conflagration, howling with laughter as the crude bombs exploded, and cheering each time a rider wheeled safely through the flames.

Toby shrank back against the curving drainpipe and looked at Sarah. He had recognized two of the riders, Mal and Whit Reardon, the men who had blinded his father.

The girl saw his dismay and his swelling anger. She pressed his hand and bent toward him with a consoling and yet puzzled glance.

"What's the matter, Toby? What is it?"

He bent away, drew his fingernails viciously across the scarred earth. "Those riders. I know them." He looked at her. "But we've got to get across."

They waited, sharing a few scraps of bread and a drink from the canteen. The dog grew restless, straining at the rope, whining softly and rubbing its haunches against the drainpipe.

What Toby saw on the other bank infuriated him: sunlight glinting on Whit's tinted goggles, Mal holding up one bare arm and making muscles, then pitching a gasoline bomb at the fire, as the other bikers screamed obscenities and laughed. Toby gritted his teeth and hunched closer to Ranger. There must be a way to drive them off.

After a while the bikers seemed to grow bored with their game. They stood around the fire, in the sunshine, passing around a large earthen jug from which they took huge swigs, spitting out mouthfuls of liquor, trading laughter and harsh oaths, and wiping their faces with the bright, coloured rags that they wore as bandannas.

"They blinded my father," Toby whispered, as if talking to himself. "I wish I had a rifle right now."

"Be patient," the girl told him, sliding down from her vantage point. "Something's happening over there."

Toby peered across.

Beyond the hump-backed bridge of cars, the bon-fire was dying down. But a fight had suddenly started. Four of the riders, including Mal and Whit Reardon, stood watching while two black-shirted bikers, locked together like copulating insects, struck blow after blow at each other, flailing and beating away as the others hooted and jeered.

After some moments, Mal Reardon stepped forward, seized one of the wrestlers by the shoulders, and began to pull him free. Whit came to his brother's assistance, as did the others, and soon a general melee was in progress. Toby noticed Mal's staggering steps, and heard the drunken language of the rest.

Now he felt Sarah squeezing his arm with impatient, excited fingers. "I'll get rid of them," she said, turning her bright eyes on Toby. "I'll make them go."

He watched in amazement as the girl closed her eyes, bent her head in concentration, and clenched her fists together.

Just for a moment her wish seemed as good as realized. The struggling bikers slowly untangled. With wobbling steps they mounted their machines. A wild revving of engines followed.

The riders took turns zooming through the sinking fire. Then an odd pause ensued. The zig-zagging motions stopped. For a whole minute, no biker moved.

Their machines still roared, but the riders hung on their seats and peered around, as if some foul wind had blown into the clearing and doused their dwindling fire.

Suddenly, Mal Reardon and the man he had pinioned earlier bumped handlebars, and a shouting match ensued.

Toby strained his ears to catch the sense of the violent exchange, but their words eluded him. Then Mal Reardon bent suddenly, slipped the sawed-off shotgun quickly from his shoulder, and held it, for one breathless instant, pointed at the heart of the other man. No one moved or spoke. He laughed and tossed the weapon to his brother.

Sarah, her body bent over and rigid, was whispering words that Toby could not catch. Her head and shoulders shook, her breath came in slow gasps. Toby was puzzled, and more than a little frightened, but he did not dare to interrupt her.

More shouting started up among the bikers, and a few angry gestures. Two of the riders leaned together, exchanging words, laughing and pointing at Mal and Whit Reardon. They shook their fists, nodded, spat on the ground. Then — as Mal made as if to charge — they kicked their machines into motion. The riders zoomed up the low rise, paused at the top of the hill for a last obscene gesture, and then disappeared. A long silence followed, except for the low revving of the engines.

*Four of them left*, Toby thought. At that moment a rider — the man Mal Reardon had challenged earlier — kicked his bike into motion. He zoomed to the top of the rise, peered over his shoulder, and seemed to gauge his distance from the river. He paused for a second, raised a gloved fist, then turned and roared back down the incline.

His machine skidded and whined. The sounds echoed across the fields of junk where the two young people lay concealed. The other bikers scattered.

Toby saw what the rider meant to do. Horrified, the boy started to spring up. He sensed rather than saw the girl's sudden gesture — and found he was incapable of moving.

Toby watched helplessly as the machine thundered to the bottom of the incline, zoomed off a small concrete ramp, and sailed up. Discs of spoked sunlight rotated beneath the rider. His body wrenched suddenly away from the vehicle and toppled backward. The bike reared riderless in the air, half turned, and splashed down in the black river. The driver smacked hard on the roof of one of the cars, bounced violently, and seemed about to follow his vehicle into the sludge. Instead, he hung there, his body twitching, his arms beating against the metal. Finally, he lay still.

Where the bike had disappeared, a few oily bubbles rose from the river.

Mal Reardon seemed to go crazy. He flung his bike into motion, zooming and swerving, first up the rise, then back toward the river, again and again, like some mechanical toy figure gone out of control.

Dirt flew, sunlight flashed wildly on metal. Mal bore down on the other two riders and sent them scattering. His tires spun, as if he would split the earth with his wheels.

Whit Reardon sprang out to stop him, his frantic screams lost in the storm of his brother's engine. A loud smacking sound, then a cry, and Whit's body crumpled, struck by the fork frame. Mal's bike tore away, hit the ramp at an angle, and was launched, with great force, toward the river. It struck the car bridge and exploded in a brief sheet of flame. Mal screamed, and, still clinging to his bike, disappeared in the dark, oily waters.

Toby, who found he could move now, turned away in horror. Sarah bent close to him, still murmuring soft invocations. On the hillside, silence reigned.

The one remaining biker dismounted and approached the river. He examined Whit's body, glancing nervously around, and shook his head, saying nothing. Finally, he mounted his bike and rode away, making for the east and following the curve of the river. The roar of his machine sounded fainter and fainter and soon became part of the steady background drone.

Toby crouched there in a kind of daze, then came to himself as he felt Sarah gently squeeze his hand. The girl stood up slowly, not looking at him, shivering inside her torn dress, pulling the slicker she had borrowed from him tighter around her body. After a few minutes her face relaxed, as if she were surfacing from some deep act of concentration.

Shrill cries from the distance made them both look up. Shapes drifted out of the pink clouds that spread away to the west, and these soon took the form of vultures, circling the car bridge at a great height and watching.

Toby let the dog off its rope and they climbed painfully over the drainpipe and walked through a rubble of broken glass and twisted metal, scrambling along the beach and then up on the roof of a battered Olds wagon, the first car embedded in the mud on their side of the river.

Close to their feet, the black, oily sludge stirred. From above came a vulture's pinched cry. The bird settled on the hill beyond the spot where Whit Reardon lay.

"We've got to bury them," Toby said quietly.

They made their way across the cars, taking care on the slippery metal, though bits of wood had been thrown down here and there to cover the most dangerous holes. The dog prowled beside them, staying clear of the water. They crossed slowly, hand in hand, and it seemed to Toby that when he and Jim White made their outward journey they had, by comparison, flown across the backs of the cars.

Three quarters of the way across their treacherous bridge, they found a mark where Mal's bike had struck, but no trace of man or machine. The body of the other rider, the one who had challenged Mal, lay spread out on the next car's half-submerged roof. His head was twisted at an odd angle, wreathed round with blood and shining bubbles.

Ranger sniffed at the body with mild curiosity and passed on.

"I've got to get a stone," Toby said. "You keep the birds away from Reardon."

They stepped carefully around the body. A vulture sat on the boulder beside Whit's form.

On the shore, Sarah wandered around, her fingers spread out as if she were tracing a web in the air. She moved toward the boulder and the bird hopped away, though another bird circled the car-bridge in a low wheeling flight.

"There's power here," Sarah called out to Toby, who was lifting a stone about the size of a man's head, tumbling it down toward the water. "The power of the serpent — they couldn't resist it. They didn't understand."

Toby straightened up and gave her a long look. He reached into his pocket and drew out the flask, holding it out so that she could see it.

"I hope there's magic in this," he said quietly. "I killed a serpent and now I have to cure my father. The bikers have been punished, but my father is still blind. If I don't help him, he ... he won't be able to see how beautiful you are."

She smiled. He gazed at her helplessly for a moment, watching her white fingers move and the birds dance away. From his pack he pulled a pair of worn gloves.

Then with an effort he lifted the stone, and, balancing carefully, staggered across the tops of the cars. He laid his burden down in the black ooze and with trembling fingers worked the zipper of the man's jacket. He tried not to look at the face, at the battered head, blood dribbling out of the mouth; as gently as he could manage he laid the weight on the man's chest, zipped up the jacket, then stood back, wiping his gloved hands on his own coat.

He tried to slide the body off the roof of the car but could hardly move it. To gain leverage he had to squat down, pressing his hands into the black ooze and shoving hard with his feet. The foul stench of the river choked him. He shuddered as his feet touched the dead man's shoulder.

At last the body stirred slightly. The boy shoved, and the dead man slid gently sideways, his right arm curled into the water. Another shove and the body seemed to float free; it balanced a moment on the surface, then, as if gently pulled down, disappeared, slipping into the oily depths. A cascade of bubbles rose, filmy and luminous, disappearing one by one as they floated away.

For the few next minutes, Toby did not speak to the girl, and hardly even looked at her. Together, they dragged the body of Whit Reardon away and hid it in a rocky cleft near the river, not far from the place of the snake. They covered it as best they could with loose stones and earth, closing the eyes that stared at them through filigree cracks in the goggles. Then they rested, throwing their blackened gloves in the river and washing their hands with water from the canteen. Neither felt hungry. The vultures, meanwhile, had flown off, and a few white gulls floated down over the glittering rubble of the Dump of Despond. When they heard the sound of motorcycle engines in the distance, but coming closer, the young people fled from the river.

# CHAPTER THIRTEEN

The afternoon wore on. They pressed northward, entering a region of overgrown fields, abandoned farms, and roads that occasionally wound through barnyards half-enclosed by the shells of tumbled-down buildings. Once or twice they had to hide, crouching in a thicket with the leashed dog, but they did not sense danger now. Even so, the jauntiness they had felt when they stopped near the fork to Apple Valley did not return, and they walked for the most part in silence, each aware of the other's occasional searching glance, but not responding, pretending not even to notice.

As they moved ever closer to the homestead, Toby's thoughts turned to his father. It seemed now that they would return before the end of the seven days, as promised by Jim White — but to what purpose? He had failed to bring back the money. Instead, he was returning with a flask of foul snake innards and a strange girl — a girl he had already made love with in the dark. But although Sarah was beautiful, and seemed kind, she had been the prisoner of Azmud; she had knowledge of things that were hidden, and Toby was afraid of her. What had she done to the riders at the river?

His father could not see, but he would sense the powers of the girl, and perhaps reject her. Yet Toby knew, only faintly, but with enough knowledge to be ashamed, that it was the girl's hidden hardness and strength, and not merely her sweetness, that fascinated him.

The day waned. At dusk they reached the railroad embankment where he and Jim had camped the first night. It had been only a few days ago, Toby realized, but that night had already receded into the far depths of his memory. It seemed now like the last night of his childhood, a mythical time, remembered from the distant perspective of the confusing present.

Toby made a pile of twigs and branches on the charred remains of Jim White's campfire, still visible beneath the dark, curving line of the embankment. They used the last of their water and made a stew of some dried meat and the greens Sarah had picked along the way. After they had eaten, they rolled out the ground sheet, warmed it awhile near the embers, and then draped it around them. They pulled off their jackets but kept their other clothes on. The girl, her light dress visible beneath the slicker, huddled close to Toby, but he twisted away, hunching up in his ragged jeans and his soiled flannel shirt, evading her, until at last she reached out and gently stroked his shoulder and arm. She took hold of his right hand, caressing it gently in the darkness.

"Toby — what's wrong?" she asked quietly. He was silent. They heard an owl hoot in the distance; the fire crackled softly beside them.

He wriggled forward in the folds of the ground sheet and pressed his face up to hers until he could feel her warm breath on his cheeks.

"I don't know what's happening to me," he whispered, unable to conceal his doubts any longer. "Who are you, anyway? I don't know anything about you. I ... I love you, Sarah. I really want you to be my wife. But there's my father ..."

She touched his forehead with her cool fingertips. "Toby, Toby," she said quietly. "I know you're upset. But you've been very brave, and you *are* my destined husband, I know that. There are some things I have to tell you, and some things I want to hear from you: how you met Jim White, and how you came to find me. We have to tell our secrets to each other. After that, we can go to your father in peace."

She encircled him with her slender arms, pressing her body against his. Her lips touched his and he felt a great calm, for his whole body relaxed with hers. It was what he had wanted, and yet feared: her gentle kiss. And when she spoke, so close to his ear, it was like a voice in his own mind, reassuringly tender and intimate, and he listened, at first without protest, to her strange story.

"My mother died when I was born," she began very quietly, "and I grew up on our farm. I never travelled anywhere, but I didn't care, 'cause I loved it so much at home — the old house, the fields, and the animals. But above all I loved waking up on the sunny mornings in my room. It was all heaven to me. My father, one of the Old Believers, told me how bad things were, about the hunger and killing, the bikers and the mutants, but our valley was isolated, and the violence didn't touch us. Not until later, that is."

She breathed deeply beside him, as if drawing strength for what followed. She continued.

"My father had sympathy for the victims, the twisted ones, the mutants. He fed them, never sent them away. When I was seven years old one of them came to stay for a while. He had a face all burned and hideous, withered stumps for hands, but he claimed the gift of prophecy. Before he left he told my father that I would be rescued from evil by a handsome young boy, who would take me for his wife. My father didn't believe him. He said the man's mind had been affected by his suffering.

"Then, when I was almost grown up, everything changed. Azmud appeared. He claimed to be a hunted man because of his strange looks and asked for shelter. My father was kind — like he always was. At first everything was all right. But Azmud began looking at me in a certain way. I got scared, but I didn't dare tell Father. I was about thirteen then. Afterwards, Brack came — the biker — with his golden helmet to hide the deformities. He'd been shot and beaten when he was young, and after that he hung out with mutants. He and Azmud used to go off together to the woods. One of my father's men found bones there, like something was sacrificed. Nobody could tell if the bones were animal bones or not."

Toby swallowed hard and pressed the girl's hand in the darkness. He did not know what to say. She continued her story, half whispering the words, almost touching his ear with her lips.

"For a while, Toby, I had suitors — seven in all. Mostly boys from the neighbourhood, some older men. They all wanted to marry me. One would appear, ask for me, then suddenly disappear. At first there were jokes about it, then everybody got confused. People said it was strange. I knew that! I was miserable. And my father began to suspect something; he challenged Azmud and Brack. I don't know what passed between them, but one day, while he was working on the roof, he had a bad fall. At the time I thought it was an accident. He died, and everything changed."

Toby did not trust himself to speak; he felt her body shift beside his. The wind stirred the fire up into a red, glowing bulb that expanded, contracted.

"The rest is like a dream, like a nightmare," she whispered. "Azmud and the other one took over the farm; everyone fled from the neighbourhood. And they made me do terrible things. They kept me prisoner there and made me do magic with them ... I ... just can't remember. Sometimes they whipped me — from that they took pleasure. Yet they said I was special, that I had power. And I do know things without trying, like back there by the river. I can do things. But I can't — I just don't want to think of what they did to me."

She clung to him fiercely. He kissed her wet cheeks until her sharp sobbing quieted. No; he did not want to hear more — not anything more! He squeezed his eyes shut and held her, as if forcing back all further questions.

They lay for some minutes, comforting one another. Then her voice came out of the darkness.

"Toby," she said. "Now tell me your story."

And he told her. It all came out — about his own childhood, his fears, about life on the homestead, about his father and the old man's devotion to burying the dead, carrying out the law for his kinfolk and for strangers alike. He told her about the Reardons and his father's blindness, about the arrival of Jim White, and the story of their journey. From time to time, when he was describing one of Jim's strange actions — like saving the snake innards, or making the dead rat disappear in the air — she stopped him, and made him go over the event very carefully.

"What do you make of that, anyway?" he asked her each time. At first she didn't answer, but when he had finished she told him.

"My father used to say that all the troubles that wrecked the earth brought the other side closer. Like in the Bible when God walked in the garden, or when the sons of God came down to visit the daughters of men ... although I didn't want that kind of visitation, Toby. I just wanted things to be like everyday. I wanted to be happy. But I'm glad you and Jim found me. Awful glad. I'm glad I could help you back there by the river."

Later, when they had no more to tell each other, the girl led him gently along, and they made love. Once again, Toby felt himself swept up into a closeness and bliss that left no room for any questions. He drifted to sleep, floating away on a rosy red light that centred at first in the fire, then spread all round him, and was in him, and as he awoke, dawn touched the leaves and the earth.

They lay there not moving, not speaking, but sharing the close warmth and listening to the birds chattering around them.

At last the dog came, licking their faces, and Toby climbed out of the paradise of the ground sheet and started readying things for the journey.

Once started, they walked eagerly until midday and reached the old concession road, only miles from the homestead. Toby's spirits leapt as he began to recognize the familiar fields of his childhood. Yet he felt uneasy, too, and anxious in his heart about the meeting with his father.

Toby and Sarah sat down to make their plans in Froats's orchard. Gnarled trunks of old apple trees rose up round them, a thin spray of branches curled into the bluish air. The sunlight, shifting down through the white clouds, warmed the earth at their feet. In the distance, a bell tolled distinctly; it was the school bell signalling the return after lunch recess, but Toby, gazing at Sarah's fresh beauty, felt that he had left his childhood behind him forever.

# CHAPTER FOURTEEN

They lingered in the pleasant orchard, talking quietly and making their plans. It was agreed between them that they would go together as far as the low hill and the pool between the boulders. From there, the path led up to Talby's cabin, and Toby would continue on alone, to carry the precious medicine, and the word of his strange adventures, to his father.

The idea seemed a good one, yet, as Sarah stretched her tired body and looked down at her crushed, soiled rain jacket and her ragged dress, she confessed to feeling doubtful. In her heart she wished for some fairy-tale magic that would transform her, bathe her weary body, and provide lovely clothes — a dress that would match the excitement and joy she felt now about her new life.

Toby tried to reassure her. She told him he hardly

understood. So they started at once, hand in hand, and their journey was brief.

When the familiar hillside came into view, Toby could hardly check his excitement. There was the pool beside the boulders, the old trees, the big clearing, the gently sloping hill path. They stood for a minute in their tracks, enjoying the peacefulness of the place. Then Toby kissed her lightly on the mouth and left her by the shining water

Climbing the hill between the pines, he looked back and saw Sarah begin to strip and wash herself in the pool. The dog, finding familiar old scents, ran ecstatically ahead.

Toby, too, sprinted forward, then stopped, and made a few perfunctory efforts to tidy his clothes. Remembering his father's blindness, and struck by the hopelessness of the task, he shrugged his shoulders and hurried along, ignoring his filthy jacket and his trousers, which, after all the rough usage, were finally unravelling and trailing ragged strips along the grass.

He emerged in the clearing, his heart pounding — and not merely from his hurried pace. Sunlight poured down on the sagging roof of the cabin. The adjoining tarpaper shed seemed to have lost several boards, but the Old Chevrolet, with its wide-open trunk and its sunken flat tires, looked almost inviting — perhaps because it was far away from the river, dumped clean and dry on the mountain, rusting away in the sunlight, amid the smell of the mint and lilac that grew round the house.

The dog ran and rolled in the garden, rubbing its back in delight on the fresh dug earth. Toby waited for his father to come out, and when no one appeared, he made his way slowly to the cabin door.

With a strange sense of foreboding the boy pushed the door back. Blinking, he entered the curtained room. There it was, just as always — the bottles piled up, the pictures arranged around the room, looking dusty as ever, and there were the old bunks and the familiar kitchen table, with Toby's own chipped blue mug sitting right in its place. But the fire burned very low in the far wall.

And then the boy cried out, for a figure rose up suddenly from his father's bunk, casting off an old blanket and shaking his white beard as he came forward.

"Toby?" his father questioned quietly, and he held out his arms. "It's you, Son, I know it is!"

The boy took a flying leap forward and grabbed old Talby hard by the shoulders. They whirled around and Talby's beard brushed Toby's mouth and his cheeks; the grey eyes, mild and loving, peered at him, unseeing blind eyes — and now he would have to cure them.

"Listen, Father!" he cried out eagerly, pulling the flask from his pocket. "I've brought medicine to cure your eyes. I killed a serpent by the river and Jim boiled the entrails. It's special medicine. Lie down right away and we'll try it."

"Medicine?"

Arm in arm, they staggered across the room to the table. Toby sat down — how strange to sit in a chair again — and the old man reached under a white dishcloth set on the sideboard and lifted up a small loaf of bread.

"You see, I've still got one loaf let. We can eat it together. But where's the money, Son? Did you get the money?"

"Dad, no ... but don't be sad! I got something better."

All of a sudden, Toby felt that he might burst into tears. The old familiar things of his childhood were reaching out to him, binding him fast with deep claims and affections he had seemingly forgotten the moment he had left the homestead. Then he remembered the slender girl by the pool, his young bride.

"Father, I have to tell you," the boy said in a rush. "John Wilson's dead. I brought his daughter."

"No money?"

His father's hands slipped from the small loaf. The old man looked at him, and far past him, with his watery, blind, grey eyes. He seemed to be contemplating something. When at last he spoke, his glance bent slightly away from his son's gaze, as if he were looking beyond Toby into the thin beams of sunlight that penetrated the cracks in the cabin walls.

"It was on the fourth night after you left," the old man said quietly. "Things were very difficult — being blind is a curse to an old man like me. I was lonely. I kept hearing shots in the distance, and I knew that I was useless to carry out the law any longer. *I might as well die*, I thought. If it wasn't for you, Son, I would have died then. So, I lay down that night in great misery.

"Well, I slept. After a long while, I slept. And then I had a dream. It was a very vivid dream, like my first dream of the angel, and I knew it must be from the same secret place. The angel — he was exactly like the angel in my first dream — spoke to me and told me that you'd come back to me. That you'd cure me and I had to trust you. In the dream I could see him quite clearly, yet I knew it was a dream, and I knew I would be blind when I woke up, so I tried not to wake up.

"Then the angel told me that there was something else: a bargain was involved. I had to agree to one thing. When my son came back — I was so happy to hear that my son would come back — I was to welcome him and his young bride. I was to send the girl a gift, a very special gift, and welcome her as my daughter. Then the three of us were to leave the homestead and go off, to settle in a new place, and start a new life."

The old man's voice drifted away, as if swallowed up by the shadows.

"Can it be true, Toby? Are you telling me what I dreamed is true?"

Toby sat open-mouthed, his mind whirling with questions. The dog poked its head through the open doorway, glanced once from Toby to Talby, and bounded up, paws thrust out awkwardly, half into the lap of the old man.

Father and son laughed together. Talby groped, broke off a bit of bread from the loaf, and fed it to the big Labrador.

"It's true, Father. What the dream told you is true."

Ranger ran off into a corner with his reward. Toby looked at his father for a minute, wondering, hoping, inwardly praying, that neither he nor Talby's own dream had deceived the old man. What if the snake potion didn't work? What would happen then to his father's faith in the power of God?

Toby took his father's hand and led him slowly over to the bunk.

"Lie down, Father, and pray with all your might. I'm going to put the snake stuff on your eyes."

The old man groaned and lay down on the bunk. "You wouldn't hurt me now, would you, Son? You wouldn't torture your own father, who's already sore tried?"

"It's got to work!" Toby said. He took the flask from his pocket, unscrewed the cap, and held it inches from his face, peering at it closely, as if he could see inside and measure the efficacy of the potion.

"By the way, Father, there's one thing you didn't mention in your story, and I'm very curious: what did the angel look like? Did he look like the angel you saw in the first dream, before I went away?"

Talby cleared his throat, coughed loudly, and rubbed his old hands together. "What did he look like? What did he look like? Why, he looked like an angel of course, all dressed in white, with blond hair and blue eyes. What else would he look like?"

Toby smiled, bent over, and very carefully poured some of the medicine from the flask into the palm of his right hand. It was a greyish liquid, and was viscous, thick as maple syrup, and odourless. But when he touched it with the fingertips of his left hand, it felt slimy and disgusting against his bare skin.

"Ready, Father?"

He moved his cupped hand quickly and dribbled the medicine on Talby's right eye. The old man groaned and started to sit up.

"Stay there!" Toby commanded. He poured out more of the liquid and rubbed it on his father's closed lids, working it in against the lashes with a gentle pressure.

His father groaned and turned away. "It's no good, that stuff! It's hurting me, Son! It feels like fire! You'll burn my poor old eyes out!"

Toby stared, horrified, as the grey liquid foamed up white in his father's eye sockets.

"No, Father! No! I don't want to hurt you."

Toby stumbled across the room to the table, fetched a small jug of water, and emptied it on his father's face.

The old man gave a shout, swung round on the bunk, and sat up. He rubbed furiously at his face and beard with the sleeve of his frayed old shirt. He shook his head, blinking, sputtering, dripping wet. He was an old man not just deprived of sight, but humiliated; an absurd figure, broken and defeated, who had somehow failed himself. He was also a man who, as Toby thought now, everyone had failed.

For long minutes his father rubbed at his eyes, blinking and grumbling to himself. Then he sniffed a few times, blinked once more, and — directing his gaze straight at Toby — said in a clear voice:

"Damn it all, Son, you look terrible! You can't go fetch no girl looking like that! You'd better get yourself cleaned up before you go back for her. I suppose she's waiting down in the woods for you."

Toby gaped at his father.

"It worked!" he screamed, diving upon the old man. They clung together, dancing around the room, knocking over the chairs, rattling the picture frames, and sending rows of the old bottles that were stacked up everywhere crashing down on the table.

"It's true, Son," Talby gasped. "I can see! Oh, blessed day, I can see!"

Toby stood by as the old man walked around the cabin, touching with great affection his battered furniture, his pictures, and his cooking implements, mumbling to himself at every step. Finally, he pushed his way out the door, accompanied by Ranger, who was now caught up in the old man's frenzied joy.

Outside, Talby cast his glance in all directions, then raised his arms to the sky in a gesture of acceptance and thanksgiving.

"Praise the Lord!" he shouted. "Praise the Lord for bringing my son back to me with the gift of sight."

Toby bowed his head. Then the old man, weeping and brushing at his face with his still-wet sleeves, came into the cabin and sat by as Toby started to pull off his own filthy clothes and change into fresh ones. The boy, ecstatic about his father's cure, was nonetheless impatient to get back to Sarah. His fears of what she was, of how his father would accept her, and how she would fit into their lives, lingered, but he took courage from her shining beauty and her strength.

Old Talby, for his part, seemed to be enjoying everything. He stood up, tossed a few sticks on the fire, nursed the flames for a minute, then began pouring water into a heavy iron dish that stood beside the fireplace.

"Wash your face, Son. Don't forget to wash your face."

Talby too, began changing into fresh clothes. As he dressed, he stood staring at his son, his lips moving to shape unspoken words, as if the sentences were being stolen from his throat before he could pronounce them.

But Toby reminded him: "You see, it was true after all, that dream of yours. And Jim White spoke the truth. And the Reardon boys, they've been punished."

He gave father a brief account of the events at the river. Talby listened, shaking his head.

"It's as we've always been, told," he said. "Violence begets violence. We have to follow the true path. We have to keep the ways of righteousness and truth."

Toby nodded, but then a thought struck him, and a question. He smiled slightly, turned away, then fixing old Talby with a sharp look, confronted him. "That angel in your second dream, Father, the dream you had the other night while I was away. Are you sure he was blond and blue-eyed, that he looked like the angel in the first dream, like the angels in the old pictures?"

Talby did not at first meet his son's gaze. He waved his hands, brushing off the question. Then finally he spoke, mumbling under his breath, and into his beard, as if he were talking to himself: "Of course I'm sure.

What a thing to ask me! I don't know what you ....
What a thing to ask!"

He bent over and scratched at his beard, silent for
some seconds, looking oddly ashamed and embarrassed.
Then with a sigh, and a shake of his head, he said to his
son, "It's not true! I made that part up. I ought to tell
the truth now that I've been blessed and cured."

After a silence, the old man continued, hesitating
a little, as if he were uncertain what had really happened and what he might have imagined. "The angel
in the dream said he was an angel all right. But he
sure didn't look like one. Neither did that angel in my
first dream either! No, sir! Both of them — and
maybe it was the same one, and a strange one at that
— looked like that black fellow that used to hang out
on the hills sometime. Top Hat, they called him.
That's what them angels really looked like. That did-
n't give me any confidence. I couldn't believe that
Top Hat could be an angel, or do any miracles for me.
I didn't want to admit it outright, but I didn't really
think that those dreams of mine amounted to much.
But I didn't want to give you any worry, Son, so I
kinda glossed over things."

Toby got up, walked over to where his father stood,
and gently took the jug from his hands.

"Jim White isn't your relative at all, Father. In fact,
he *is* old Top Hat, the man who roams around in the

woods. But don't let it worry you. I guess you see a lot of things better now, Father."

Talby threw up his right hand in a gesture of frustration. "Gosh darn it, Son, how was I to know who he was or what he was? I wanted to tell you my dream so that you'd believe it! I guess Jim White, or old Top Hat, or whoever he is, did what he had to do in the way that was best for us all. Now don't be asking me if I believe in dreams or in magic, because I don't. I believe in the Law, that's what I believe in. And I believe you're going to lose that girl if you don't go fetch her right away."

Watching his father lay out the table, setting out the cheap knives and forks, the glued-together crockery, Toby knew that it was no use discussing the mysteries with the old man. Talby might be an Old Believer, he might talk to angels in his dreams, but he also moved through an everyday world, and through the unchanging world of the old faith, happy with the things he knew and trusted. He grew fearful and suspicious when mysteries thrust themselves on him.

Sarah Wilson, though, was different. Sarah seemed to know things, to be in touch. Toby had the feeling that he was destined to be drawn, through Sarah, into the deep spaces of life. He felt resigned to this, and excited, yet at the same time, afraid.

And suddenly an image of Azmud, with his long, clutching fingers, came into his mind. Quickly, the boy reached down and splashed his face clean with warm water.

He was soon well-scrubbed, dressed in fresh old jeans and a worn but clean plaid shirt, and wearing soft canvas shoes. He was attempting to inspect himself in the cracked bit of mirror that served as the two men's small vanity when his father came up to him carrying a thick bundle, all wrapped in layers of ancient newspapers and tied up with odd bits of half-rotten string. The old man — Toby wondered why he looked so sad — deposited the parcel in the boy's arms.

"Take this, Son. It's for your new bride."

Talby turned away, and the boy knew it was time to leave him, to let his father prepare himself further for the changes, the new life.

Ranger had finished his morsel of bread. He lay by the door, whimpering softly, and scratching at the old scored wood. Toby shoved the door wide open and the dog sprang out, running straight for the trees, then scampering away down the hill.

Toby smiled. He would walk back much more slowly, savouring every second of his approach to the lovely Sarah.

# CHAPTER FIFTEEN

The girl bent over the pool, her bare arms moving in the sunlight. She splashed at the water; it ran cold and clear on her skin. She felt happy, free for a moment from old cares and new anxieties. The big boulders were reassuring, the air in the woods clear and light.

There had been few moments like this in her life, almost none in fact, until Toby came. A few years before, she had fallen into a lethargy, overcome with sullen resentments, nearly paralyzed with a fear of the unknown powers that surrounded and controlled her. Now the knowledge that she was at the beginning of a new life stirred her. A mild and pleasant expectation, a wary kind of happiness, possessed her. She stopped splashing in the pool long enough to let the waters settle, and looked down at her own image, liking the face that she saw there, aware of her youth and her beauty, feeling as if she had just been born all over again out of a darkness she didn't dare to think about.

The image of her dead father, faint and half-imagined, seemed to hang at the edge of her consciousness. The remembrance touched her, but she didn't want to let it come any closer — that would have been too painful. As for Azmud and Brack, they evoked only a shudder. Toby must never know the real power they had over her. She would never give in to his curiosity, never even think of, much less tell him about, the dark rituals they had brought to her father's farm.

Sarah pulled back from the pool, shook the water droplets from her bare arms, smoothed back her hair, and looked down at her half-ragged clothes. She imagined old Talby's scorn at her waif-like appearance — he would expect her to be perfect for his son — then remembered that the old man was blind.

She sat down, resting her back against one of the boulders. Birds sang around her, a squirrel darted away up a tree trunk. She closed her eyes and dozed for what seemed only minutes.

Suddenly, she awoke. Her eyes opened wide and all of her senses told her at once that the atmosphere of the woods had changed. She felt the difference in her blood, on her skin. The birds were completely silent; the bushes and branches barely stirred. Sunlight poured down as before, but now it seemed harsh and heavy, as if, while she slept, some secret, sour passage of time had contaminated it. She hardly dared breathe or move.

A figure walked out of the woods. He stopped, looked at her, smiled a short ghastly smile, then stumbled on in her direction.

The man's body was wrapped in filthy leather rags. He was bare-armed and bald-headed, his face smeared with dirt and blood. He walked hunched over as if with the weight of something terrible; one of his boots was missing. His expression, stiff with pain, fixed his face in a stoical mask, yet she recognized him at once.

It was Mal Reardon.

The biker's steps swished in the high grass. She couldn't move. She wanted to run but she could not. His eyes held her. She clenched her fists and waited.

"You!" he growled at her. He stopped in his tracks, swaying a little. For a moment she thought he would fall down. "*Bitch*! *Demon*!" he murmured, almost under his breath, and he came toward her.

Suddenly, in her mind, she was back in her father's barn, face to face with Azmud and Brack, being shouted at and bullied, forced to obey their commands. The clearing around her filled with darkness — a darkness in her mind and memory, one that the sunlight could not dispel.

"You're the one!" the man croaked at her. "I watched you from the river! You have the power — just like the mutants!" She could see the beads of sweat on his forehead, patches of leather, soaked and singed, that clung to his lower body. A bare knee, sticking out from the shreds of a trouser leg, seemed smashed or broken, and one side of his face was horribly burned. In his right fist he held a short metal tube.

He had escaped the terrible crash — she could hardly believe it. She struggled to reassure him, to meet his threat with sanity, but her words came out in a forced whisper that betrayed her terror.

*"You're hurt! You need looking after."*

The man was now within twenty-five feet of her. There he stopped, fought off a fit of coughing, and spat out some blood. He shifted the metal tube in his right hand, his fingers moving nervously across it. It was almost as if, unconsciously, silently, he were fingering a flute.

She remembered how she had danced to the sounds of Azmud's instrument. Danced before the Ark of Evil. She felt ashamed and horrified at what she had brought into her own life and the lives of others, yet she was conscious at the same time of her innocence, of how she had been violated by the designs of the evil powers.

"I can help you," she told him. "There's a cabin nearby. Someone's on his way — he'll be here any minute. We can take you there."

She cast a quick glance over her shoulder. *When will Toby come?* She must run away, intercept him, warn him that Mal is still alive.

"Take *me* there?" the man sneered at her. "Oh no, you won't take *me* anywhere. I'm taking *you*, and not far. Oh no, not very far. Just into the woods there. Where I want to go. Where we can have some fun, you and I. One of my mates is waiting back there in the woods. He brought me here, helped me trail you, so I could find you."

Mal took a step forward. Sarah looked at him, fixed her mind, all her thoughts and powers, attempting to set up a psychic wall between them — an invisible, impenetrable barrier. Slowly, with great difficulty, the man tried to raise his right arm, but failed. It was as if a terrible weight held it down.

"Bitch!" he screamed. "Don't try your foul tricks on me!"

His face twisted in agony. He paused, his body shaking with the effort to move toward her. Then he stopped. His eyes gleamed with triumph.

In a great, loud voice, a voice with a power that belied his hurt body, the man cried out: "Azmud, O Great One, help me to defeat the woman!"

His words evoked horrors; they seemed to penetrate deep into Sarah's mind. He had called on her own master to defeat her! Images from the past flashed before her — terrible memories. *The blood of innocent animals running over stone. Human heads hung up in the sky. A white face in the darkness of a barn.* She swayed in her tracks and collapsed on the ground before Mal Reardon.

Reardon laughed, raised his lead pipe, and advanced on her.

A crashing of brush, a streaking form, a fierce animal breathing ... and the dog Ranger was on the man. Reardon toppled backwards, rolled across the turf, swung his weapon, and caught the animal on the snout. Ranger's shrill cry filled the clearing.

Sarah struggled to her feet. Another man, a burly biker in shining black leather, had walked out of the woods. In his right arm he cradled a sawed-off shotgun, and he swung the weapon from side to side as he swaggered toward the fallen Reardon.

The girl ran to where Ranger lay, took the dog's head in her hands, and, between sobs, brushed away the blood from the animal's muzzle.

"Need some help, partner?" the second biker laughed. "I'll finish the bitch and the mutt together."

He raised his shotgun and waited for the signal from Mal Reardon.

Mal climbed to his feet and said: "Kill the dog, but I want the girl for myself."

The second biker laughed and walked over to where Sarah held Ranger.

"Move away," he commanded, but Sarah only clung tighter to the dog, stroking Ranger's neck, her eyes closed, her lips moving in a whispered prayer or curse.

Toby ran into the clearing, stopped in his tracks, and took in the whole scene. He saw the crouching Sarah and the wounded, whining Ranger. And Mal Reardon getting to his feet, while the second biker leveled his gun at the girl and the dog.

For an instant, paralyzed with horror, the boy could neither cry out, nor move a step from where he stood. It was then, in that suspended instant, caught between unthinkable alternatives, that he saw something else. Not only Sarah, Ranger, Mal, and the second biker, but well beyond them, at the edge of the woods, another figure. A familiar one, standing motionless, his back pressed against a tree trunk. A man — or something like a man — dressed in rough traveling clothes and wearing an incongruous, quite ridiculous, black top hat.

"Jim White!" the boy cried.

The second biker whirled toward Toby, raised his shotgun, and fired. But Toby jumped aside just in time. Sprawling helpless — but unhurt — on the grass, he heard the deadly whine of the bow, and saw the second biker leap up suddenly on his feet and then fall forward, an arrow piercing his neck.

Mal Reardon screamed, staggered up, and took a second arrow in the front of his throat.

The bikers lay unmoving on the grass. Jim White walked slowly from the shadows of the trees. Toby ran over, embraced Sarah, and helped her to her feet. The piteous Ranger, bruised a little, bleeding, and whining softly, accepted the comforting ministrations of Toby and Sarah.

"Looks like I timed it just about right," Jim told them. "You young folks do seem born for trouble!"

# CHAPTER SIXTEEN

"Jim, you found us! You came back! What happened to Azmud?"

Toby was beside himself. Just when everything seemed to have settled down, his world had exploded again. He had wandered from his father's cabin, taking his time, caught up in a youthful dream of ecstasy, imagining the sight of Sarah by the pool. Then came Ranger's piteous cries, and a mad dash toward the clearing. But if Jim White had not been there ...

Jim stood, sweating and grinning, casting a few wary side looks at the two men he had killed. It was just as if he were really old Top Hat, the crazy man of the woods, and not what Toby was beginning to suspect, or imagine, Jim to be: a messenger from on high.

"Your young lady's all right," Jim reassured him. He pulled Sarah to her feet. "I'm pleased to see you again," he told her. "After Azmud and I parted, I thought it might be wise to follow you two, just to make sure you made it home all right. Now, I have something else to tell you."

Sarah nodded and managed a smile. She wiped Ranger's blood on her ragged dress, and embraced her rescuer.

"My father's cured!" Toby blurted out. "He can see! And I did it with the snake innards you saved for me! But he had a dream, Jim. You were in it. At first he pretended you weren't .... I don't think I understand anything."

Jim White laughed.

"He's an old man. It's hard to cure an old man's blindness. But you did well, Toby. Very well."

Jim's face wrinkled up in amusement, and Toby noticed a long white scar that marked the big man's forehead, a scar that hadn't been there before they stalked Azmud at Wilson's farm. Jim saw the boy's look, and anticipated his question.

"It was a struggle, and that's a small memento. Something to think about until the next time. But evil doesn't rest, not in this world or any other. It doesn't die, either; if you're lucky, you can push it back a little — that's about all."

The big man paused and looked around the clearing. "I have something to say to you two — some advice to give you. But first, let me see to that dog."

Jim White bent over Ranger, cradled him for a moment in his arms, then examined the raw wound on the dog's muzzle. He murmured a few words under his breath, touched the animal on the top of its head, and stood up. The dog lay there, not moving, panting heavily. Jim walked over to the pool, cupped some water in his hands, and gave the dog a drink. Ranger settled back, eyes half closed, tail wagging.

"He'll be all right," Jim told them. "Now sit down here by the boulder and listen to me."

Toby and Sarah settled down beside Jim, who carefully removed his battered old top hat and laid it on a stone outcropping beside the big boulder. Sweat ran on his scarred forehead; his grizzled hair shone in the afternoon sun. Jim White fixed his dark eyes on the young people and began to speak in a slow, solemn voice, occasionally emphasizing a point by means of a gesture of his big hands.

"You have to understand. Azmud isn't dead. In a sense, he can't die. This world isn't cured of its troubles, either, and won't be for some time. There are still mutants and gangs of bikers — friends of those two lying there, and just as bad. The law is still violated every day. Don't make any mistake; word of what happened here will get out. Sooner or later the bikers will come after you. Now, here's what I want you to do."

Toby took hold of Sarah's slender hand and listened.

"I'm heading out right away. I'd like to stay and help, to drop in again on your father, Toby, but I have other things to do. It's not in my hands, really. But you take Sarah up to meet old Talby. Tell him what happened. Then come back down here and bury these two — I know Talby will want to do that anyway. Sarah, you'll be all right at Talby's — leastways for a little while. But all of you have to pull up stakes as soon as possible. It's time to break with the past. You remind Talby that I said that, Toby. I want you to take the old man to Apple Valley. The bikers have no power there — not yet. But don't stay there very long, because there's another place, out on the coast, that you have to get to as soon as possible. That's a land of promise where many ordinary folks, and some of the Old Believers, are heading. It seems that kindly men from the far eastern lands, monks and Zen masters, have settled there, and are starting to cultivate the land again. They want new settlers. They want good people. There's a chance out there, a chance for a new life. It's up to you to take it — for the sake of the old man ... and for the sake of your children."

Jim paused; Toby squeezed Sarah's hand and waited. But Jim seemed to have no more to say. He stood up, looked around the clearing, shook his head at the sight of the sprawling dead men, put on his old top hat, and turned to the young people with a smile.

"Well, I'm off," he said.

They clung to him for a few seconds, wrapped their arms around the big man, endured his gentle grunting protest, stood back as he detached himself, smiling, from their embraces.

"Walk safe in the world," Jim told them. He turned away and strode off across the sunlit clearing and into the shadows of the big trees.

For some moments, Toby and Sarah stood there unmoving. Then the girl turned, took Toby roughly by the shoulders, and kissed him.

They had questions for each other, much to talk about. But first, there were things to do.

"I've got to meet your father," she said, "and just look at me!"

Toby tried to reassure her. "You look just beautiful," he said, but he could see that she wasn't content with that. Then he remembered the parcel — and it struck him all at once what his father might have passed along to Sarah.

"Wait a minute! I've brought something for you!"

He ran back, fetched the bundle from the place where he had dropped it, and thrust it into her hands. While she tore away the strings and paper, he delivered a few words of explanation about what had happened at the homestead.

Dust beams floated in the sunlight; there was a flash

of white cloth and she tumbled it out: a white dress, all ribbons and soft flowing frills of sheer cambric. A long dress for a wedding.

The girl shook the dress gently, running her fingers through the soft folds.

"Your mother's?" she asked, looking sharply at Toby.

Somehow her manner of questioning made him feel uneasy.

"I guess so," he said quietly. He had never seen the dress before — never wanted to, for fear of the hurt it would carry — though his father had often told him about it.

"I like it," Sarah said quietly. She smiled at him. "Now, Toby, you go on up the hill, past where those pines are, and wait for me there. I'll come along in a few minutes."

Obediently, with a tender, awed look at the girl, Toby started off.

"And don't you dare spy on me!" she called after him, already fussing with the old-fashioned combs she had found packed with the dress.

He went on, without looking back, and when he got to the top of the rise where the pines clustered, he plumped himself down, resting his back against a slender tree trunk He sat there in a dream, studying his own rough footprints in the cleft of the trail and wondering if he would ever see Jim White again. He was beginning to think that dealing with a woman was no easy thing.

It seemed to take a long time, but at last he heard a movement behind him on the trail. Did he dare to turn around?

"Come and help me, Toby Johnson," Sarah's clear voice called out to him "And if you tell me I look silly ...!"

Toby stood up. The girl approached, moving between the sunlight and the shadows, her bare feet pressed down on the pine needles.

Frills and white ribbons flowed around her; her white shoulders rose from a cascade of shimmering fabric; her dark hair, gathered up, framed her face, emphasizing her cheekbones and the deep-set beauty of her eyes. With one hand she held a length of the gown, as if she were ushering herself along up the hill.

Stunned by such simple, clear-shining elegance, seeing that somehow, within a few minutes, she had made the old dress her very own, so that it might well have been crafted just for her, Toby leaned forward, and, with a heart full of admiration and tenderness, gently kissed her hand.

Then he led her proudly, step by step, up the path toward the homestead, eager for his father to look on her, eager to show old Talby his new bride.

### The End

## A Note on *Demon in My View* and the Biblical *Book of Tobit*

*Demon in My View* is based on an earlier story of mine, called simply "Book of Tobit," which was published in the collection *Strange Attractors* (Beach Holme, 1991).

The original *Book of Tobit* first appears in the Septuagint Greek version of the Bible, compiled around 150 BCE in Alexandria, Egypt. Although not included in the later versions of the King James edition (1611), *Tobit* appears consistently in Roman Catholic editions, notably in the Douay (English) Bible in 1582. *Tobit* is, in fact, one of the Apocryphal Books (apocrypha = hidden things), which were not admitted as canonical by the Jews, because they were not thought to have been originally written down in Hebrew. (A fragment of the *Tobit* story in Hebrew, however, was discovered a few decades ago at Qumran, among the Dead Sea Scrolls.)

The story itself is an immediately appealing and memorable one, and it has charmed readers and inspired painters and illustrators through many centuries. It embodies the (partially first-person) account of Tobit, a pious Jew in exile in the city of Nineveh, who — although a functionary of the Assyrian King Shalmaneser — takes it upon himself to violate the local laws and bury the Hebrew dead in the Assyrian land. He is exposed and ruined, but restored after

Shalmaneser's death. Shortly after this, a worse misfortune strikes.

One night, because he is ritually impure after a burial service, Tobit cannot return home. Instead, he sleeps in the open air and is blinded by sparrow droppings. Thereafter his wife must go to work, and when she is given a bonus — a goat — by her employer, Tobit grows irrationally suspicious and feels it may be stolen property. They quarrel, and Tobit is miserable and even prays for death. At this point we learn that his young kinswoman Sara, who lives in Ectabana, another Assyrian city, has also suffered great misfortune. She is very beautiful, and has attracted no fewer than seven suitors, but one after another of them has been killed by the demon Asmodeus on the night of their wedding to Sara, which has caused her to despair of life.

God finally intervenes, dispatching the angel Raphael to earth to help the two families. Tobit remembers a sum of money owed him by someone in Ectabana and sends his son Tobias to collect it. Raphael pretends to be one of Tobit's kinsmen and accompanies the young man. They depart, accompanied by Tobias's dog. Beside the Tigris River a large fish tries to swallow Tobias, but he catches it. Raphael advises him to save the heart, liver, and gall. When they reach Ectabana, Tobias falls under the spell of Sara and becomes yet another bridegroom. This time, however, the demon is defeated, because Tobias — as instructed by the angel — burns the heart and liver in the bridal chamber, driving the demon away. Once the marriage is consummated, Asmodeus has no power over them. They return home, Tobias treats Tobit's eyes with the fish gall, and the old man's blindness is cured. Raphael announces himself and departs. Tobit lives to a ripe old age. Tobias prospers, and although he departs from Nineveh, he lives long enough to see its destruction by the Medes and Babylonians.

A story that tells of a pious but suddenly blinded old man, a dutiful son, a beautiful young woman, an angel, a demon, and a dog — how could it fail to be memorable? A wonderful narrative, yet the Biblical style in which it is related is anything but pictorial, and seems to cry out for visual elaboration. No wonder painters such as Raphael, Rembrandt, Fillipino Lippi, Perugino, and the modern master Balthus, among others, have been moved to render it.

As many commentators have noted, the Tobit story is also rich in echoes from traditional folktales. The figure of Asmodeus the demon, who plagues Sara on her bridal nights, falls into the general folkloric category of "the monster in the bridal chamber," a common one the world over. This type of tale should be distinguished from a superficially similar one, known as "beast marriage" story. The latter occurs in well-known fairy tales such as "Beauty and the Beast," and "East of the Sun and West of the Moon." Unlike the "beast" who in such tales seems destined to marry the heroine, the "monster in the bridal chamber" is not necessarily the spouse, but an evil being that, for one reason or another, threatens the bride. Many traditional marriage rituals and superstitions exist because of this ancient fear that the bride is especially vulnerable to evil, and perhaps likely to be "devoured" before she can take up her new state. Both types of story embody the notion of the severity of the rite of passage from sexual innocence and single life to marriage, and while they may be rooted in the sometimes fearful experience of traditional brides who were pledged to give themselves almost blindly to husbands unknown to them, they continue to be relevant to many aspects of modern marriage, still an exciting, difficult, and sometimes daunting stage of relationship for young people.

But what of Asmodeus? Because Sara is so beautiful, she is plagued by this demon of lust and wrath. In short, her beauty turns her suitors into raging demons, burns them up, and destroys them as enduring husband material even before they can connect with her, whereas the kind and gentle Tobias woos her in a more calculated fashion. It is significant that — as Raphael explains — once the marriage is properly consummated "the demon" is powerless. The burning of the heart and liver makes a "sweet smelling" incense for the wedding night, soothing the newly married pair, curing any incipient frenzy, and routing Asmodeus, just as in the *Odyssey* the hero Odysseus's "moly" plant charms the beautiful witch Circe, and the pungent garlic, in eastern European folklore, drives off vampires.

The folkloric motif of the "grateful dead" is also present in this tale. Tobit's burial of the dead earns him their gratitude — an important point, because in the "monster in the bridal chamber" stories, it is often intervention from "the other side" that routs the monster. While there is no direct intervention of the "grateful dead" in Sara's chamber, the burning heart and liver can be seen, not just as a nostrum to drive off the demon, but as an offering to invisible guardian spirits, who make it impossible for Asmodeus to kill Tobias, although it is Raphael who pursues the demon to Egypt and binds and shackles him there.

Raphael, one of the well-known angels of Hebrew mythology, appears suddenly from "the other realm," the "beyond," but takes human form. He is exactly parallel to one of the "grateful dead" just mentioned who, in many tales, having been given proper burial by the hero, or otherwise benefitted, come from the other side, in human guise, to join him on his quest. Such a companion not only often helps the hero solve some impossible task (in this case defeating the demon and curing Tobit's blindness), but usually assists him in winning a fortune, which of course the honest protagonist offers to share with his benefactor — at which point the disguise is revealed.

Because of my love for the Tobit narrative, I decided to rewrite it, removing it from its Biblical context, but retaining the folkloric and mythological connections. I see it as a great family story (although in my version the mother is missing), and as a mythic or fantasy structure with rich implications. The father and son relationship, the meeting of the rather innocent young man with the more experienced young woman — I found these subjects fascinating, and was even more intrigued by the mysterious companion of the hero, who may or may not be an angelic visitor from the other world. Also, the addition of the dog in the Biblical narrative, a delightful touch, seemed to cry out for elaboration.

In my version I make some major changes. Above all, the narrative becomes more ambiguous. Most of the time we seem to be in a world that, however debased, operates like our own — according to familiar natural laws. But sometimes, by intention, my Tobit world veers toward the magical and the fantastic. The beauty of myth and folktale is that they can carry various levels of reality, various kinds of truth in a single story.

In terms of details, I transform the kinsman companion of Tobias (Toby) into a black man not related to the family, give the dog a name and character, and substitute a snake for the large fish in the Biblical version, and the snake's entrails and venom for the fish's heart, liver, and gall. I present the demon Asmodeus in the form of the evil mutant Azmud. Toby's "treasure" in my story is not material wealth, but the love of a beautiful girl. I imagine Sarah as much changed and transformed by her contact with evil, however, and see her as much more powerful and active than her Biblical prototype. As for Tobit, after his blindness is cured, he is still learning how to see.

My biggest change, however, is to place the story in an imaginary Canada of 2099. The world of the Biblical Tobit is uncertain, dangerous ... and so may our future be. It might even be primitive, chaotic, and ruled by violence.

Science fiction and dystopian romance often work their way "back to the future"; that is, they render the world to come not as a technologically advanced, but as a primitive realm, or — as in my story — as a post-historical era, in which most of the viable social structures have collapsed, and social order is threatened by arbitrary violence and lawlessness. From the perspective of 2006, we can — sad to say — easily imagine such a future. We can predict attacks on the developed countries, and on North America in particular, by terrorists and rogue powers. We can be sure of the increasing rise of militarism and the worst kind of mindless jingoism. We can foresee an irresponsible use of sophisticated weaponry, and a failure of confidence in authority, followed by the breakdown of all central governmental power. Thereafter gangs and warlords may well arise to take the place of the legally constituted authorities, and we may be certain that complex technologies and mass communications would hardly survive this. In fact, we can visualize the destruction of most of our workable infrastructures. We can predict the growth of frightening religious cults, especially the chiliastic (Second Coming) ones, and the triumph of superstition.

Even today, we are threatened by new plagues and pandemics, by active terrorism, and by the polarization of contrasting fanaticisms. (The philosopher Santayana once defined fanaticism as "redoubling your effort when you have forgotten your aim.") Our environment is under assault by pollution and global warming, and the economic gap between rich and poor is growing alarmingly. Who is to say that the future could not see a breakdown of many social structures we think of as secure, and that a plunge into chaos and violence is impossible?

Many of us are baffled and fearful. Have the bright hopes that cheered the world after the end of the Cold War vanished before they could become reality? Have the diverse and rich human societies of planet earth missed their best chance to work together for the benefit of all? Can we still chart our future course so as to preserve the precious biosphere we must all share? If we cannot deal creatively with the problems that are so clearly visible in the first decade of the twenty-first century, our real future may not be very different from the one I have depicted here.

What I have hatched here is a story of adventure, camaraderie, and love, but as in the original Biblical *Book of Tobit*, a seemingly inescapable social and moral dimension makes itself felt. I would be very happy if readers, and especially young readers, after enjoying this tale, sat down and asked themselves some searching questions.

Tom Henighan
Ottawa, 2006